A DEFENDER RISES

A DEFENDER RISES

MAGIC CITY CHRONICLES™ BOOK ONE

TR CAMERON   MICHAEL ANDERLE   MARTHA CARR

DISRUPTIVE IMAGINATION™

LMBPN Publishing
PMB 196, 2540 South Maryland Pkwy
Las Vegas, NV 89109

First US edition, January, 2021
ebook ISBN: 978-1-64971-400-8
Print ISBN: 978-1-64971-401-5

Beta Team

Larry Omans, James Caplan, Kelly O'Donnell,
John Ashmore, Rachel Beckford, Allen Collins

Thanks to the JIT Readers

Dave Hicks
Deb Mader
Wendy L Bonell
Peter Manis
Jeff Goode
Allen Collins
Dorothy Lloyd
Diane L. Smith
Jeff Eaton
Angel LaVey
Misty Roa
Larry Omans
Paul Westman
Kerry Mortimer

If I've missed anyone, please let me know!

Editor
Skyhunter Editing Team

DEDICATIONS

For those who seek wonder around every corner and in each turning page. And, as always, for Dylan.

— *TR Cameron*

To Family, Friends and
Those Who Love
To Read.
May We All Enjoy Grace
To Live The Life We Are
Called.

— *Michael*

CHAPTER ONE

Ruby shook her head in annoyance as she watched Jennifer flounce through the crowd toward the restroom. *Meeting her at all was stupid enough. Meeting her here, though, that took some special effort at being dumb. Well done, Ruby.* She sighed and finished off her Ringer, a Pilsner from a craft brewery on the other side of Nevada. She made eye contact with the bartender and pointed at the two empty glasses. The tuxedoed woman behind the long metal-and-stone bar nodded.

Any of the wide variety of casino bars on the Ely, Nevada Strip, which resembled a mashup of the one in Vegas with Fremont Street in that city, could have hosted her reunion with her high school frenemy. Since the other woman offered the invitation, it had seemed only right to let her choose. Still, Ruby hadn't expected Jennifer to select the one gambling hall that would have easily won the award for "Most likely to piss Ruby off." *Then again, that's exactly the way she would have acted six years ago, so it's probably stupid for me to be surprised.*

Looking around at the place, she had to admit that the

Sunshi family had done a beautiful job with it. It was soft and elegant, all whites and golds and blues, making one think of the sky, mountains, or the oceans. Each of the casinos in Ely, Nevada was owned and operated by a different group of magicals, earning the town the nickname Magic City. It wasn't as big as Las Vegas to the southwest or Reno to the west, but what it lacked in size it made up for in originality. The Mist was one of two gaming establishments owned by members of the reclusive Mist Elves, who had remained hidden from everyone on the magical planet of Oriceran for generations upon generations until finally, the allure of coming across to Earth proved too strong to resist. Ruby's family owned the other one, called Spirits.

None of the other magical groups had more than one casino. Her family and the Sunshis were the exceptions because they'd founded the kemana beneath the city in years long past as a home for the Mist Elves on Earth. She'd been in each of the other casinos many times but still liked her family's best.

Ruby looked down at her watch with a frown. This reunion had already gone longer than she'd hoped it would. It was her first time back in town in nine months, and although she'd seen her family a month before when they'd visited her in Massachusetts for graduation, she would have preferred to see them before having to cope with Jennifer. *Another dumb move. Glad I'm getting them out of my system all at once. Well, I'll get to see the fam soon enough.*

She plastered a fake smile on her face as the other woman returned from the restroom. As Jennifer slid into the seat next to hers, the bartender put their fresh drinks in front of them. Ruby nodded her appreciation at the server's care, which eliminated any chance of the beverage being messed with while its owner was away. It was one of the many little things that made visiting Magic City a unique experience compared to the state's other gambling destinations.

Jennifer had attracted the attention of almost everyone she'd passed on the way back. *She'd fit in much better in California than she does here.* She was blond, blue-eyed, thin, and her cheekbones could still cut glass, just like in high school. Hoop earrings dangled under her long hair, and she wore a gold chain with a rhinestone "J" on it. Her white blouse was cut deep enough to entice the eyes, and her tight jeans were no doubt intended to do the same. Ruby's jeans, t-shirt, and leather jacket didn't begin to compare.

They'd been sometimes friends and sometimes competitors in high school, and the other woman remained unaware that Ruby was a Mist Elf. Instead, she thought her an adopted daughter of the casino owners, as did almost everyone else who knew her. Camouflage, illusion, concealment—these were things Mist Elves excelled at, and keeping secrets was part of their very essence. Jennifer sipped her drink and flashed a wide smile. "So, tell me all about your degree. Some kind of computer thing, right? Took you long enough."

Always needling. Ruby fingered the golden sun pendant she constantly wore. In places like this, where anti-magic emitters protected the games from interference, having a magical backup for her disguise was always a good thing. It was also the only reason she could do any magic at all without letting her illusion of being a perfectly normal human fade. It would permit her to "accidentally" knock Jennifer's drink into her lap with a small burst of force without revealing her delicately pointed ears or the tattoos that would appear when she summoned her power. *That would be wrong. For some reason I can't quite think of right now.*

Ruby sighed inwardly but kept her expression neutral. Carelessly displaying her emotions would never do. "No, not computers as such. Engineering. Electromechanical and Magical."

Jennifer gave a small, sympathetic frown. "It must be difficult, being part of a magical family but not being magical yourself." It reminded Ruby of why they'd fallen out on more than one occasion. Still, something about the other woman remained stuck under her skin to keep them connected. *Like a parasite, maybe. Wonder if there's a medicine for that.*

"You don't have to be magical to work on magical devices. You only need to know how to collaborate with magicals. That was one of the main things we did during the years I worked on my master's degree." *Ha. Take that.* Jennifer had stopped at a bachelor's degree, preferring to jump into the working world. By all accounts, she was blazing her way up the corporate ladder at the travel agency that exclusively served Magic City. Still, graduate school was one thing Ruby had accomplished that the other woman hadn't.

"Who would have thought our Ghost would be so highly educated?" She delivered the line with a thin smile, but Jennifer clearly believed the old nickname still bothered her. It wasn't particularly inventive despite Ruby's pale skin, light eyes, and almost white hair. Combine that with the name of her family's casino, and it became down-right predictable.

A standard deflection reached her lips but didn't get past them. Instead, the sight of six human-sized and -shaped figures approaching the large cashier window about twenty feet away from where she sat caught her attention. The way they moved had snuck into her subconscious as a warning. They strode through the crowds with purpose, all of them heading on direct lines that would converge at the three windows that served as the casino's cash exchange. Two paralleled the wall that held the cage, and the other four marched through the lanes between the gaming tables, pushing past magicals and non-magicals ranging from gnomes on the short side to Kilomea at the opposite end of the height spectrum.

She thought to shout a warning to the ubiquitous casino guards as the bombs went off. One was behind the bar, and she was too slow to save the bartender. Her force shield snapped into place only an instant before the flame and debris reached her chair. Ruby had the reflexive presence of mind to wrap Jennifer in her protection, and they both flew backward, propelled by the energy that hit the shield, and tumbled onto the main casino floor. Once things stopped falling on them, Ruby pushed on Jennifer's shoulder to keep her down and rose with a snarl to take stock of the situation.

The thieves—their march toward the casino cage left little doubt what they were—had set the stage cleverly. Detonations had occurred in numerous locations spread across a wide area, to judge by the smoke and the shouting, and the casino's guards logically moved to deal with the

injured. Her rational brain observed that damaging innocent magicals from multiple species wasn't a smart move
unless the criminals wanted the whole town against them.
She stored the idea away for later as water poured out of
the sprinklers and sent chills through her as it slipped
down the neck of her black leather jacket.

Her first instinct pulled her toward helping the injured,
like the security personnel, but she was concerned about
the people in the casino cage. Not the money—any casino
that didn't have the appropriate amount of insurance to
cover themselves against such things deserved to be taken
for all they were worth simply for being bad at business.
However, the criminals had already shown a willingness to
wound or kill, and the Mist Elves behind the bars of the
cage would have their magic blocked by anti-magic emitters. Even magical casino owners didn't possess an abun-
dance of trust in their employees, especially ones
proficient in illusion.

Weapons emerged as the figures closed on the cage,
black pistols that looked like the 9mm ones she'd used at
the shooting range near her university. Ultimately, what
kind they were didn't matter as much as their presence,
and that the people they threatened couldn't use magical
defenses against them. Fortunately, the thieves were still
outside the cage and far enough away from the gaming
tables that there would hopefully be a gap in the defenses
against magic use. She half-stumbled toward the wall while
pretending to be more stunned than she was until she
drew close enough to act but remained far enough away
that they might not notice her doing so.

Ruby had practiced martial arts since childhood. She

worked her way through the human versions first, then specialized in the Mist Elves' art, which incorporated magic as a fundamental element in its most effective form. Because she'd attempted to stay disguised, and performing magic caused her illusory humanness to falter, she'd learned to use it with and without invoking her powers.

She knew getting involved was a risk, both to her safety and her ability to continue the pretense that she was human. Still, she couldn't not intervene. Ruby had never been one to stand by and do nothing. She'd have to hope that the amulet she wore would be sufficient to cover her magic use. She also hoped that she'd be up to fighting at six-to-one odds long enough for someone to come and help her.

Her eyes narrowed as the first man to arrive yelled insults at the workers behind the counter and demanded that they fill the bags he and the others threw at them. The workers looked at the manager, who nodded, and his people began to empty the drawers. For a moment, she thought they might all get out of it without further incident. Then the first thief demanded, "And the drop safe. Now."

The manager stammered, "We can't open it. That's the whole purpose of a drop safe." His skin was even lighter than Ruby's, offset by dark hair and eyes, and a sharp business suit concealed his thin body.

Another of the criminals laughed. "I'm going to start counting. Whatever number I get to before that safe is open is how many bullets are coming your way when I run out of patience." He smiled. "One."

The manager went even paler. "No, really. None of us can do that. Only our bosses."

The other man's grin widened. "Two."

Ruby realized that whatever was going on, it wasn't only about the money. The purpose remained unclear, but their actions weren't consistent with the goal of getting out with the cash. She frowned at the scene. As water from the sprinklers dropped from her bangs into her eyes, she realized that she had the perfect way to even the odds, and if she was lucky, take out the bad guys without a fight.

Stretching out her senses, she pictured a line of force connecting the men's gun hands, then brought it to life and attached it to the power outlet nearest them. The water pooling in the channel she'd created carried the energy along it, and all the men dropped their weapons to avoid electrocution. She huddled against the wall and tried to look unimportant, but one of them must have noticed her motion and decided she was to blame for the strange occurrence. He pointed at her. "I'll deal with this. You deal with her."

The remaining five walked toward her. Three of them drew collapsible batons from their pockets as they came. The other two rushed at her as though they'd tackle her.

Guess today's not my lucky day. Time to make sure it's not theirs, either.

CHAPTER TWO

Ruby spread her stance and turned so she didn't face the oncoming men head-on. A step away from the wall gave her room to move. No one around seemed to take an interest in her or the would-be thieves, so she resigned herself to dealing with this flock of morons on her own. The hard part would be keeping her use of magic subtle enough that she didn't reveal her true nature to Jennifer if she happened to be watching. Something inside told her that would be a bad idea for all sorts of reasons.

I should never have agreed to pretend in the first place, but when you're young, and your mother and father tell you to do something, you do it. Now that it's all built up into a big thing, I can't risk messing with whatever they're up to. She knew her parents would have had a long-term strategy in mind, way back when—Mist Elves didn't make any serious decisions without considering the implications over at least decades, and usually centuries. *Long lives will do that for you.*

Regardless, she'd avoid using magic if she could, in case her amulet was too drained to keep her disguise going.

Non-artifact magical items demanded lots of care and attention, and in the move home, she *might* have given it a little less than it required. *Or a lot less. It's kind of a blur.* Her time for thoughts that didn't involve combat ended as the first man arrived.

He and the second guy had clearly worked together before, as they'd widened out sufficiently that she couldn't easily defend against them both at the same time. Against an untrained person, the tactic might have been alarming enough to be effective. However, she'd trained in fighting groups in several of her arts. It was familiar enough to be comfortable. She faded to her left, putting the nearer man between her and the farther one, and swept her arm in a graceful arc to intercept the jab he threw toward her face. Her open palm caught his wrist, lifted it, and pulled it forward as she dipped her head out of the way. Her upward punch slammed into his locked elbow and destroyed the joint with a *snap* and a scream. She stepped back and kicked him into the other man who'd arrived second, then backpedaled as the ones with batons sought to encircle her.

Her sparring partners almost always underestimated her at the outset, as the initial attacker had. A couple of would-be muggers who'd tried her over the years had fallen into the same trap. Now she saw in her assailants' frowns the realization that they'd encountered someone worthy of at least a modicum of respect. The nearest one whipped the baton at her ribs, twisting to put the power of his approach behind the blow. She spun away from it, only to find another of the weapons slicing downward at her head as she completed the first revolution. A step inward with her nearer foot reduced the area he could strike, and she grabbed his wrist, pulling the weapon down and past her. She chambered her knee and drove a kick back at the first one who'd swung at her, and he stumbled backward.

She didn't surrender the man's wrist but instead yanked his arm up, spun underneath it, and used her leverage to force him to flip to avoid having the joint broken. Ruby snapped a kick that drove the toe of her heavy boot into his temple, and his eyes rolled up in his head. She dove forward as she sensed someone at her back and narrowly avoided a baton strike. The weapon passed close enough that it ruffled her hair. She fetched up against one of the gaming tables and felt the pressure of the anti-magic emitter as it tried to suck away the magic she was using to disguise herself. The amulet snapped to life as she pushed off the furniture to get out of the emitter's range.

The Mist Elves' illusion skills were more than capable of evading the efforts of low-end anti-magic emitters, given how intertwined the powers were with their very existence. Unfortunately, gaming tables usually featured the heavy-duty models, which would rapidly drain her backup concealment option. She flowed out into the wide aisle that separated the gambling area from the former bar she'd enjoyed her beer at only minutes before and turned to face the remaining attackers. The one who'd been unarmed had retrieved the fallen baton, which was something she'd hoped to do.

The element of surprise had allowed her to take out the first two quickly, but the rest of her enemies advanced warily. *Damn it. They look like they've done this before.* The groups she'd fought in martial arts practices often had the same attitude. *No way around it. I'll need my magic to give me an edge. Just have to hope for the best.*

Mist Elves based their fighting style on the elements: the planet's surface, for solidity; the air, for acrobatics; water, for the ability to flow where danger wasn't; and fire, for quick and devastating attacks. She ran toward the centermost opponent on the assumption that his partners would be less likely to attack if he was in the way. The man set his feet and swung the baton like a baseball bat, throwing all his force into a blow that would have crushed her chest if it had connected.

It didn't, of course. She'd planned for his actions and gave herself a boost of force magic to assist her jumping flip over him. Ruby grabbed his neck as she rotated over his head, then used it to throw him as she landed. A slight twist added to the move would have broken it, but she resisted. Her training taught her to kill if necessary, but she didn't judge it so at the moment. She spun immediately, lifted her left arm vertically in front of her torso and face, and wrapped it in a cocoon of force magic. It intercepted the strike that one of the men aimed at her head, but she felt the shock of another impact her leg before it crumpled underneath her.

She threw herself to the side in a roll to avoid the follow-up strikes. Her leg went from numb to needles and pins as the blow to the nerve bundle started to wear off. However, she was a prime target while on the floor, and the men circled to either side of her. She scrambled backward in a crabwalk but had to abandon it as the one on her right aimed a blow at her knee. Ruby yanked it back and caught the strike on the sole of her boot, then snapped out a weak kick at the man's knee. He skittered back, and it gave her the opening to roll away from the other one's attack at her head.

She used another burst of force magic to lift her from the floor and send her spinning horizontally into the backpedaling opponent. He went down under her, and she made sure to stomp on his weapon hand as she pushed herself back to her feet to face the other one. Belatedly, she realized she'd lost track of the man who'd overseen the theft while the others dealt with her. The bullet that burned through the top of her left shoulder provided an agonizing reminder of his presence and location. Muttering a litany of swear words her family would be properly shocked to hear spill out of her mouth, she ran at the remaining one with the baton while weaving to avoid getting shot again.

She stretched out a hand and used a tendril of force to bring one of the fallen batons to her. It slapped into her palm in time for her to use it to deflect a downward strike from her foe. She circled, and he did the same in the opposite direction, apparently not realizing she was trying to bring him into the last one's line of fire. *Nice when they're not entirely competent. Although these are pretty good, all things considered.* A flick of her wrist tested her opponent's defense, and he smoothly intercepted the baton tip headed for his face with his weapon, then countered with the same move.

Ruby leaned back to avoid it, then spun to the side as he stepped forward. At the moment his balance shifted, she snapped a kick into his knee. The blow lacked the force to break the joint, but it was sufficient to compromise his footing. She spun in reverse and whipped her elbow around at his face. The shock of impact occurred earlier than expected as he deflected her strike, and she instinctively swept her arm down in a block that intercepted the sidekick he launched at her ribs. They were too close now for batons and traded quick punches and kicks, blocking with forearms, shins, and feet.

She clenched her jaw at the dual realizations that her opponent was well-trained and the wound in her shoulder slowed her down. She relaxed her control and let her natural magic flow from her, creating a veil over her fist as it traveled toward his face and an illusion of the incoming attack a half-foot to the right. He reflexively moved to block the danger his senses perceived, and the punch connected. He stumbled away from her and dropped his baton in surprise. She leapt into the air and delivered a flying sidekick to his chest that knocked him sliding backward.

With the attacker down, the first man came into view again. He was lifting his pistol now, pointing it at the people behind the bars of the cage. She had no time for finesse and no way to intervene without calling upon her magic. She clapped her hands in front of her, and a wave of force rippled out from them, directed at a downward angle to hit the floor before it reached the innocent cashiers.

It was still in full effect when it struck the man with the pistol and propelled him forward into the bars of the casino cage with the strength of a team of horses all kicking him at the same time. The cracking sound as his bones broke carried over the bedlam in the casino. He crumpled, and she met the eyes of one of the Mist Elf women in the cage, who gave her a respectful nod.

The adrenaline left her, and Ruby staggered to a nearby wall and slid down it to the floor, the throbbing in her shoulder suddenly overcoming all other sensations. She put her head down, the long platinum hair occluding her face, and focused on solidifying her disguise again. Moments later, there was nothing left to suggest she was anything more than a regular human caught up in the crossfire.

Nothing but the gazes from behind the cage bars that kept returning to her. Ruby shook her head. *I definitely shouldn't have let Jennifer pick our meeting place.*

CHAPTER THREE

Ruby must have lost focus because the sudden *thump* and groan that accompanied Jennifer sliding down the wall to sit beside her almost made her scream. She pushed down the instinctive response and shook her head. "Damn, woman, you should warn a person."

Jennifer snorted, then coughed. The casino's ventilation system was still working on the dust and tiny debris created by the explosions. "I called your name a bunch of times. Not my fault you zoned out." She pushed a hand back through the tangled mess that her previously perfectly straight blond hair had become and scowled as it got caught. "I missed almost everything, I think. I spotted you as the guards blasted the last guy with magic."

Ruby blinked, then nodded to cover her surprise. "Yes. It's good that the guards stepped in." Her parents had always taught her that people tended to see what they expected, which offered a decided advantage for a group that used concealment and disguise as naturally as hers.

"Did you hear anyone say anything about what the point of this was?"

Her friend shrugged. "Looks like a robbery to me. I mean, what else could it be?"

Ruby shook her head. "If it was a simple cash heist, these people were way dumber than they seemed. You'd be better off doing that almost anywhere than in Ely. Hell, it'd be easier to steal from a casino on the Vegas strip, and according to *Ocean's Eleven*, no one other than George Clooney or the Rat Pack has managed that, ever."

Jennifer rolled her eyes. "I'm not positive that basing your opinion on a movie is the wisest choice. They teach you that in grad school?"

"Ha. Ha." A shadow falling over them deflected the witty retort that Ruby was sure would have immediately leapt into her mind. She looked up to see a powerful-looking woman standing next to them, dressed in a County Sheriff's uniform: lots of brown fabric set off by metal, leather, and plastic in black. The officer was solid. The muscles at her biceps and thighs pushed obviously against the outfit, but she still looked like she'd be fast and light on her feet. Sizing up opponents at a glance was one of the things all her martial arts teachers had considered important, so Ruby had a lot of practice at it.

The woman's voice was unexpectedly relaxed, given the gravity of the circumstances. "Hello, ladies. Hold on a second." She turned and shouted, "Paramedics, over here, now." A man ran up to her after only a couple of moments, and she pointed. "Looks like a shoulder wound, at least. Check that out." She went down to one knee so she'd be more or less at eye-level with them. "So, I'm Sheriff Alejo, and I'm overseeing the situation here. Seems like you had a front-row ticket."

Now that Ruby wasn't craning her neck to see the other woman, she noted the slight wideness to her face, the darkness of her long hair, which had been pulled back into a professional braid, and the thin black eyebrows above her brown eyes. She looked like someone who'd be happy to welcome you into her home for a party but would be equally comfortable bodily throwing you into one of her cells if you caused trouble. Ruby replied, "Yeah, it got pretty exciting there for a minute."

Jennifer interrupted, "I didn't see too much, but I think the bar blew up in our faces. Oh, no, is the bartender okay?" Her face fell as the reality of what had happened finally broke through whatever defenses she'd used to hold it at bay.

The sheriff shook her head. "Afraid not. A few didn't survive the attack, mostly those unlucky enough to be positioned right by one of the bombs."

Ruby frowned. "Only a few? That's good, but what was the point of the explosives if not to kill people?"

Alejo's eyes came to rest on hers, and she read suspicion in them, but not specifically directed at her. *Yet, anyway.* "Seems like they used them as a distraction rather than to inflict maximum damage. There were a lot of easy ways they could have been much worse."

"Sounds like experience speaking."

She shrugged. "Twenty years in the Army, you see a thing or three. Let's get down to the important stuff. The other people I've interviewed said they saw a white-haired woman fighting the attackers. I presume that's you."

Ruby nodded. "Yeah."

"Why? What do you care about the casino's money?"

Dust tickled her nostrils, and she sneezed into her sleeve, then sneezed again as she inhaled the dirt smeared on it. When she'd collected herself, she answered, "I don't, although if they wanted to give me some as a reward or something I wouldn't say no." The joke didn't cause even a ripple of amusement on the other woman's face. "It looked like they were going to hurt the workers in the cashier area. I couldn't let that happen."

Alejo nodded slowly. "Even though it was one against six."

She shrugged. "I've done martial arts for exercise pretty much my whole life, and part of it has been fighting when the odds aren't even."

A chuckle escaped the other woman. "Odds. Even. Casino. I see what you did there." She brushed a stray hair off her forehead, and Ruby could picture her tipping back a cowboy hat, or maybe a sheriff's hat, with the same motion. *I bet she's all "Aww shucks" right up until the moment she punches a bad guy's lights out for him.* She shifted her gaze to Ruby's left. "And you? Notice anything different?"

Jennifer shook her head. "No, I didn't see much. The explosion threw us backward, and I was groggy for a while. When I got up, Ghost was fighting, then one of the guards blasted everyone."

"That tracks with what others have told me. By 'Ghost,' you mean your friend here, right?"

Ruby interjected, "It's a high school nickname. You know, from a time when we were much less mature." She glared at Jennifer. "Ghost was nicer than Casper, anyway."

The sheriff straightened with a low groan. "I can see that. My skin and hair got me called 'Dusty' until I beat down enough people to convince them to stop saying it."

"Maybe I should've adopted that approach."

Alejo chuckled. "Never too late to start. Seems like you have the skills to make it happen."

Ruby let out a long exhalation. "Honestly, I don't know what came over me. I guess getting blown up made me mad. Caused me to lose connection to my brain or something."

The woman towering over her called a name, and a uniformed man stepped into view. "This is Richardson. He'll get your specifics, along with some contact information in case I want to have another word with you later." She ambled off and the paramedic, who had been working on Ruby's shoulder the whole time, spoke.

"It's a deep graze. I have it packed up, but you should visit a hospital or urgent care for further care. We have people who can't move under their own power to take care of." It wasn't a denigration, merely a statement of the moment's reality, delivered with a note of apology.

She smiled at him as he rose. "No problem. Thanks for taking care of it. Already feels better." It didn't, but that's what a normal, polite person would say, and she did so although she was neither.

As he moved away, Jennifer observed, "He was cute."

Ruby sighed. "Really? Now?"

Her maybe-friend shrugged. "Might be he wants to go to medical school. You could do worse than marrying a doctor."

She closed her eyes. "Not in the cards."

"Cards. Casino. Hah."

"Yeah, I'm a laugh riot." She mustered her energy and pushed backward with her feet, sliding her back up the wall to stand. The room wavered a little but then steadied. "I need to get home. I'm going to grab the tram over to my folks' place." A ground-level monorail connected all the casinos in a large loop, and all residents of the town had free access to it through a small key fob or smartphone app.

Jennifer rose as well. "Want me to come with?" Her tone suggested she didn't want to, which wasn't a surprise. She was pure human, as far as Ruby knew, and the rest of Ruby's family were visibly not. It made some people uncomfortable and made others intrigued. Only a narrow band in the middle took it in stride, and most of her high school friends weren't part of that segment.

She shook her head. "No, I'm good, thanks." They parted with a hug and a promise to get together again, and she wondered if Jennifer shared the opinion that it would be some time before that particular commitment was honored. Then she was free and moving toward the rear of the casino. As she passed the cage, a cashier gave her a small bow. He'd twisted his fingers into a symbol she recognized, one of the easiest to identify among the physical version of the Mist Elves' language: "Thank you." She touched her eyebrow in recognition, "Fare well," in the same language. As with many of their words, it had a dual meaning. In this case, both a goodbye and a wish for health and fortune. Accompanied by a certain facial expression, the context would flip and it would become an insult. *As much as we're like humans in many ways, we're unlike them in at least an equal number.*

She headed toward the tram but turned away when she was near the back of the casino and walked down an unmarked hallway. A tingle of magic was the only thing that distinguished it from countless others along the way. At the end of it lay a blank wall, but a murmured spell and a wave dispelled the illusion long enough for her to find the button that opened the door and press it. She slipped inside and closed it behind her. A railing surrounded a wide rectangular hole in the floor, easily twelve feet on the long side and ten in the other direction. A circular staircase descended through the opening for those without the requisite skill set for the preferred means of travel.

She leaned over the railing and saw only darkness. The black metal of the steps disappeared in the lack of lighting. She grinned, leapt over the banister, and fell into the endless black.

CHAPTER FOUR

Of course, the darkness wasn't *truly* endless. It only seemed that way from above. She kept her body vertically oriented with small bursts of force magic against the shaft's stone walls. Dim lights inset into those walls indicated her depth, counting down to the bottom. When three showed, she pushed force magic underneath her. At two, she increased it, and at one, she killed her velocity enough to land softly on the ground. She quickly stepped forward, vacating the passageway for the next person who needed it. The illusion at the top would have prevented anyone else from entering the room while she was dropping, but it never hurt to move rapidly after landing, in case.

The kemana that lay under Ely was one of the most recently constructed, about a century old, give or take. The Mist Elves had created it for their use at first, unlike many others around the country that were intended from the outset to be shared among all the Oricerans in a given region. Its architecture and design reflected that fact. It was about twice as large as the city atop it, built in an almost perfect oval except where a natural feature that broke the shape was deemed beautiful enough to maintain, like the rock formation that resembled a lion near the easternmost point of the cavern.

Kemana MountHaven was shaped a lot like the athletic stadium she'd visited for several football games while in college. The "field" area was oval like the rest of the space. In the center of it sat what looked like a modest castle, the home of the kemana's titular leader, the "Lord" or "Lady" depending on their preference. A small street ran around it; also an oval, and spokes shot out from it to the edges of the bowl, intersected along the way by two more oval streets, these double the width of the central one.

Tiers climbed the incline above the bottom, occupied by shops at the lowest level, then homes whose size got smaller as the stairs to access them rose higher. At intervals, the terraces were slightly larger to provide for narrow single-lane ring roads that encircled the area. The landing spaces for the casinos' shafts all exited onto the same tier, which held only the vertical tunnels and a walkway to reach the stairs. Portaling to one's home was always an option, but Ruby figured a short walk would help clear her head before dealing with her family. Plus, a healer along the way could see to her shoulder, and much better to have that done before her siblings and parents judged her for being at that particular casino in the first place.

Purple crystals adorned the ceiling and combined with the soft white orb that hung directly over the palace to throw a warm glow over the hustle and bustle of the magical underground town. The structures were mainly of stone and wood, with metal primarily for decoration. The

Mist Elves had a connection to nature on Oriceran, and brought that philosophy to their home on Earth. Ruby strode confidently toward her destination, the healer's shop located on the lowest tier, conveniently more or less along the path from her current location to her family's home. She could see the house in the distance, larger than the ones around it by at least half, as befit her family's status as one of the kemana's founders. Her parents had been among the first Mist Elves to relocate to the human planet once crossing became possible.

That was probably the reason they wanted me to appear human, their spy to collect knowledge of those who might turn out to be enemies. I guess I should consider it a compliment. Still, it seemed a heavy burden to put on a child, if one was the child in question. She reached the healer's shop and gently knocked on the door.

It swung wide to reveal a large open reception area with a single being sitting in a tall chair. The bespectacled gnome in a formal purple robe who occupied it looked at her over the top of the book he'd been reading. He smiled upon recognizing her. "Ah, if it isn't my favorite jewel."

She laughed as she stepped inside. "Challen, you're such a flatterer." At a gesture from him, the door swung closed behind her.

He chuckled and climbed down from the chair, using the footrest set into it as a step. "I see you're favoring your left arm. Let's move into the back." He led the way to his healing room, which had a cushioned table for her to lay upon surrounded by a raised platform that would permit him to walk around at the right height to examine and help her. "Okay to cut this?"

Ruby nodded. "The EMT already stretched the hell out of it. Do what you need to."

He snatched a pair of scissors from a nearby tray and sliced a rectangular hole in her t-shirt to access the wound. He cleaned then used the same scissors to clear away the bandages the paramedic had applied and made a clucking sound. "Whoever packed this did a good job. We can do better." He laid his palms on it and whispered under his breath, and a wave of warmth and pleasure replaced the pain that throbbed from the wounded area. Healing by laying on hands was a rare talent that cut across cultures in both planets' history. To have a practitioner in the kemana was hugely beneficial to the community. Unlike most who lived in MountHaven, he'd been invited to relocate there and was paid a retainer to stay that allowed him to live in comfort, which was all he seemed to desire. Well, that and help with his experiments.

That was how they'd met for the first time. He'd needed someone to collect a particular plant on the surface, and her parents had suggested she should do it since she wouldn't attract notice in her human disguise. He, of course, knew she was a Mist Elf and not a human. Few others in the underground city did. She had tokens and items to explain her uses of magic if it became necessary to do so and was known to be a member of the Achera family by most everyone she encountered. Down here, the air held so much power that she could maintain the disguise without worrying about the power cost and did so automatically.

When Challen lifted his hands, the injury was partially healed, reduced to an angry scarlet line and a lingering ache. He jumped down and told her to get up, then handed her a small flask filled with a dark red liquid. "Healing potion. Drink it tonight before bed. It will do the rest of the work once my magic wears off."

She grinned. "What if I decided to take it now?"

He frowned. "You'd be insufferably rude."

A laugh escaped her. "I believe I've heard you describe me that way on more than one occasion."

He nodded. "Never truly. Only in jest. If you were to do it anyway, the combination of my healing magic and the healing potion would make you feel amazing, until you tried doing something with the arm that *should* have hurt and injured it again. Pain is a teacher. Heed its lessons."

Ruby sighed. "All right, all right, you win. Anything you need done around here? Small tasks I can help you with?"

The gnome waved a hand. "No, no, I'm good. It's part of my work for the kemana." Then he gave her a shrewd look. "Ah, you're procrastinating, aren't you?"

"Of course not."

He laughed, the sound like a chime in the small room. "Off to see your family, then?"

"Gotta go. Been nice seeing you." She opened the door and headed out.

He called behind her, "Have fun, Ruby! Be sure to convey my greetings to your parents." He was still laughing as she closed the door, perhaps more loudly than strictly necessary.

Everyone's a comedian, she grouched as she stomped toward her home. It was one of the few located at the cavern's bottom since only the founding families were permitted to live among the more extravagant shops that filled the base layer. A high stone wall surrounded it, warded and protected against intrusion by any uninvited guests. The magic at the gate recognized her and allowed her entrance. The defenses snapped back into place the moment she passed through. *No doubt they announced my arrival to everyone and anyone who happens to be inside.*

That assumption was confirmed as the large double doors that served as the main entrance to the house opened, revealing a tall, thin Mist Elf in a formal robe in her family's silver and blue colors. A grin spread across his visage, showing brilliantly white teeth. He could have come from central casting with his perfectly upswept ears that ended in delicate points, the long hair that came down over his shoulders, and the perfect face structure. Not for the first time, she wondered if Peter Jackson had met with a Mist Elf before working on *The Lord of the Rings*. He hadn't captured the elegance, but he'd gotten a lot of the rest of it right where her people were concerned.

"Welcome home, Miss Ruby."

She walked up to him and wrapped her arms around him, pressing her cheek to his chest as he returned the hug. "It's good to see you again, Matthias."

He laughed. "And you. It's only been months, though."

She disengaged and smiled up at him. He was several inches taller than her, and she'd always suspected he wore lifts in his shoes to give him at least one of those inches. Despite investigating, she'd never been able to confirm it. "Yeah, but now I'm back for real, not for a visit."

He nodded. "We will be glad to have you back, believe me."

Ruby lifted an eyebrow. "The others being annoying?"

Matthias leaned in as if sharing a closely held secret. "No more than usual."

She snorted and followed it up with laughter. "So, everyone hopes that I'll calm things down, is that it?"

"Perhaps, Miss. Perhaps. Also, you're just in time."

She frowned, having totally lost track of the hours. "For what?"

"Dinner."

Ruby groaned, and the older man grinned. "Maybe you should change clothes, though. Those are a little…dusty."

She looked down at herself, covered in debris from the explosions, plus a few telltale drops of blood on her jeans from being shot in the shoulder. She acquiesced with a sigh. "I suppose you're correct, as always."

Matthias smiled wider. "Right this way, Miss Ruby. I'll ensure you remain unseen until you're ready to be seen."

She shook her head and followed him, wondering if the most painful part of her day was over or whether it lay in her immediate future. *No one knows how to push your buttons like family.*

CHAPTER FIVE

Her bedroom at the family house still had all the trappings of her childhood. Stuffed animals sat across the pillows on her large canopy bed, the middlemost a three-foot-high brown bear that had been taller than her on the day it had been gifted. Her furniture was all off-white wood with silver fastenings and handles, a wardrobe, a dresser, and a vanity with a mirror. She'd spent many hours combing out her hair in front of it, both in her human disguise and in her true form, and dreaming of what the future might hold. The memory brought a smile to her lips, and she pulled out the drawer and saw that the wide brush she used was right there waiting, like always.

The family had five full-time employees: two cooks, someone who specialized in cleaning and taking care of the house, a jack-of-all-trades, and overseeing them all, Matthias. Of them, only the last knew her humanity was an illusion, so she had to maintain appearances even at home. It wasn't a burden per se, merely something to keep track of. *Fortunately, I don't have to live here full-time anymore. Only visit. A lot.* Her parents would doubtless have been fine with her returning. Her siblings, far less so. While she loved them all and had missed them terribly while she was away, being able to get some distance when she needed to was always a good thing.

She shrugged out of her clothes and threw them in a backpack she found in the wardrobe, then removed a pair of jeans and a thigh-length tunic from the dresser. The top was dark blue with a wide patterned stripe down each side set with silver studs. She pulled her hair back into a ponytail and tied it with an elastic recovered from her vanity. To the woman in the mirror, she said, "You got this. It's only family. Can't be worse than fighting off a bunch of bad guys and getting blown up, right?" She laughed at her dramatics.

The other Ruby didn't look convinced. *Ha. What do you know? It'll be fine.* She left the room, walked down the long hallway that connected the house's wing to the central structure, and took the switchback staircase down to the first floor. Matthias waited at the bottom and nodded in approval. "That color looks lovely on you, Miss Ruby."

She laughed. "You'd say that regardless of what I wore."

He shrugged his elegant shoulders. Not a strong man, her instincts told her, but he'd be fast. She'd be shocked if he wasn't a trained fighter. While it had never come up, her parents would be foolish not to have their employees be able to act in defense of their home, and if there was one thing her mother and father weren't, it was foolish. "That doesn't change the truth of it."

"Well, thank you, Matthias."

She made a slight move in the direction of the front

door, and he interposed himself with a grin. "The dining room is the other way, Miss Ruby. Perhaps you've forgotten?"

Ruby scowled. "Traitor." She braced herself, lifted her chin, and marched toward the battlefield that was the family meal.

Her brother's voice carried down the hallway as he argued over something. At first, it was unintelligible, and she didn't care enough to amplify it magically. As she neared her destination, his words became clear. His tone was arrogant, almost demanding, which wasn't one she'd use on her parents without an excellent reason. "It's a simple concept. Marijuana is legal in the state. We can push the legislature to extend that to drugs that have a similar influence on magicals, then use the casinos to distribute. It's foolproof."

She lingered outside the door to listen as her sister Morrigan replied, "Dralen, you're an idiot. It has the potential to bring in the kind of clientele we don't want in there." Their responses perfectly fit their ages. Her brother was twenty-two and working on his MBA, which meant that he was always thinking of business ideas but not quite ever turning them into business plans. *It'll be good when my parents are ready to step down, though.* She had no interest in being in charge of the casino, although she'd help where she could. Morrigan, at eighteen, was done with high school and taking a gap year. She wasn't sure what she wanted, but it apparently included continuing to block Dralen where she could. Ruby approved.

She stepped around the corner as her mother said, "No business at dinner, you know that." They were gathered at a rectangular table that could seat six with her father on the end, Dralen on his left, and his wife and daughter on the right. The dining room was typical of the house itself with light stone walls made of big blocks, wood furniture in either white or natural brown, and accents of color in fabrics and ornaments. The table was a wood so dark it was almost black, with a runner of blue and silver down the center and placemats in the same shades at each chair.

She slipped into the seat next to Dralen in silence and looked up at her father. "What?"

The recipient of her question, Rayar Achera, was entering the latter part of his adult life, and his brown hair was now liberally sprinkled with grey. That didn't take away from the animated energy in his eyes or the twitching grin he bestowed upon her. He put a hand on his heart as if in shock. "Prodigal daughter. You've returned."

The others at the table laughed. Her mother, who like part of many long-term couples was growing to resemble her partner, scowled. Sinnia's hair echoed her husband's, long, straight, and shot with grey. Her face was a little wider where his was noticeably narrow, and her frown had an edge of sincerity. "Ruby. We thought you'd join us earlier."

She shrugged as she reached for one of the serving dishes in the center of the table, then put off her answer until she'd scooped some of the rice-cheese-and-vegetable entrée onto her plate. "I was unavoidably delayed."

Dralen nodded. "By Jennifer, right? How is your old friend?" He made air quotes around the word friend. The pair had dated for a while and now fell solidly into enemy camps.

"Yeah. Meeting her was dumb. She hasn't changed."

Morrigan asked, "Did she call you Casper?" Ruby had shared all her important stories about life with her little sister, including how vicious alleged friends could be.

"No. She did manage to work Ghost in there a couple of times."

"What a witch."

Ruby laughed. "Or something that rhymes with that, yes. At least that obligation is taken care of for the near term."

Her father asked, "Will there be a long term?"

She chewed and swallowed. "Answer unclear. Check back in a year or so." That drew a laugh, and she continued, "So what's happening here, other than another terrible business idea from Dralen?"

Her brother sputtered, and her father came to his rescue. "It takes a lot of misses before you hit a home run. At least he's in there swinging." He flipped his fork like a bat to illustrate his point.

Ruby met Morrigan's gaze, and they rolled their eyes together, laughing. Her sister replied, "Don't worry, big brother. One day you'll make contact with one of those pitches." She paused with perfect timing, then added, "Sure, it'll be a pop fly right back to the pitcher, but you know, at least you'll have hit something."

Her mother changed the subject. "Did you get all your stuff back to town okay?"

She nodded. "There isn't that much of it. The U-Haul is over at the house. If I'm lucky, my roomies have unpacked it for me already."

"I don't know why you want to live up there instead of with us, anyway."

Ruby laughed. "Mother, I'm twenty-five. It's time for me to not live with my family. Besides, you know, we *humans* love the sunlight." Referencing that secret never failed to end an argument. Sure enough, her father changed the subject.

"What are your plans? Still the same?"

She shrugged. "I have some contacts from school in the area. I'll see if they have any freelance work for the near future. Eventually, I'd like to open a place, making and selling magic items."

Rayar nodded in approval. "Ambitious. I like it. You'll continue to help your mother and me, and your brother and sister, with the casino, of course."

"Naturally. Can't be an Achera and not have a hand in Spirit."

"Good, good. Perhaps you and your brother will come up with some fantastical new way to use magic for gambling. That would be truly useful. Imagine the franchise opportunities." He wandered off on a tangent about the cost of slot machines with popular brands, and she tuned out and thought about her future in a way she hadn't before returning home. It was all real now. She was out of school, ready to make her way. Unlike many, she had one hell of a safety net in her family, but if all went well, she'd be able to do what she loved and put her spare time to use volunteering to help others in Ely, as she had those in her college town.

Morrigan's voice brought her back to the present. "Did you hear about the thing at the Mist?" She went on to talk about the explosions and the attempted robbery so that whether the family had heard about it or not, they had all the details by the time she finished. Ruby figured she had zero chance of hiding her involvement, so there was no point in lying. *Thanks, sis. Couldn't have waited until I left, huh?*

"Yeah, Jennifer and I were there. The bar blew up in our faces. Fortunately, I had on a shield amulet and activated it quickly enough that we didn't get hurt." A little lie, in case any of the staff other than Mathias was listening.

The others turned to look at her, and her little sister's eyes narrowed. "Wait. I saw on Twitter that a human woman fought off the thieves. It was you, wasn't it?"

Dammit, Morrigan. Shut it. "Yes. I was never in any real danger."

They all spoke simultaneously, and finally, her father's voice rose to the top. "Why did you get involved? Who cares if the damn Sunshis gets robbed? If they don't have insurance, they deserve it."

She laughed inwardly at the echo of her earlier thought. "Because the thieves looked like they were going to hurt the people working the cashier cage. I was in a position to help. Admittedly, it turned out to be a little harder than I'd expected."

Her mother's frown deepened. "Are you hurt?"

Ruby shook her head. "No. Well, I got shot, but it was only a graze, and Challen fixed me right up."

Again they talked over each other, and again the patriarch's voice finally won out. "That was extraordinarily stupid, Ruby. You are *invaluable*. You have to take care of yourself."

There it was once more, her mysterious importance to the family that they never explained. She had many theories. At that second, she figured it was a business strategy they'd hoped to use to make the humans like them more when she was a child, which then went wrong. At other times, she imagined they might have been trying to normalize closer relations between humans and the Mist Elves, who were always considered reclusive. Sometimes she pushed, but never got a good answer. They'd always deflected until she'd gotten tired of asking and accepted the situation with at least a touch of grace. Mostly.

The voice in her head that was generally critical of her observations suggested, "Well, you're twenty-five now. Perhaps the response will be different." Although the humans saw twenty-one as the line that separated a child from an adult, it was a quarter-century among her people. *Maybe. I'm not interested in having that conversation right now.*

Ruby shrugged. "I'm fine, the bad guys lost, and it's all good. Now, how about we all enjoy a meal together without antagonizing the 'prodigal daughter'?"

Dralen grinned. "I think that's a great plan. Let me tell you about this fantastic idea I came up with for a giant roulette wheel that the gamblers use force magic to spin." As his words droned in her ears, Ruby pasted a smile on her face and enjoyed the food. It was the best part of the situation, other than making faces at her sister. *Thank heaven I can leave here when the meal is over. My roommates will probably be annoying sometimes, but they can't hold a candle to my relatives.*

CHAPTER SIX

Ely's main area was devoted to casinos and hotels, much like on the Las Vegas Strip. *Tourist-land.* A few high-priced condos lay among them, but that wasn't the sort of place that she could legitimately afford, even with her family's comparatively deep pockets. She wanted to make it on her own, give or take the occasional meal at the family house or an unexpected gift from her parents. *Just like anyone.* She kept her eyes locked on the passing sights as she reclined in the back of the Toyota sedan. The town glittered with neon and lights like stars in the early evening twilight.

She'd found her roommates online. They'd gotten to know each other virtually after deciding they had the right group but had never all met in person. The prospect of doing so was daunting. Still, they had a bunch of things in common. One of them was a witch, and Ruby had spent a lot of time discussing a lab setup that would serve them both. The plan, signed off on by the others, was to set it up in the basement. In return for ownership of the space, they would get the least desirable rooms, up on the third floor in a converted attic. They both thought that was an eminently fair arrangement.

As she exited the autonomous vehicle steered by magic, she stared up at her new home. The big old house held three other bedrooms, all on the second floor, plus a dining room, living room, and kitchen with a laundry room attached on the ground level. Two and a half bathrooms for the five of them, barring sleepover guests and the like, would make showering and getting ready potentially annoying depending on schedules but not impossible. Her lab partner Daphne had a just-past-entry-level job at the casino run by wizards and witches in partnership, the Ebon Dragon. The wand-wielders in Magic City numbered fewer than any of the other magical groups, for reasons no one had ever shared in her hearing.

A small lawn in front of the house struggled to be green in the arid climate and mostly failed. She walked up the sidewalk toward the narrow porch and the door, wondering who she'd find inside. The other three boarders were male. The one she liked best so far, Demetrius, was a dark-skinned wizard whose aptitude was in infomancy. His wand was replaced by or incorporated into his computer rigs. He'd agreed to pay a premium share of the electric bill, and the cost of high-speed internet, which out in the desert wasn't an inconsiderable charge. His smiling eyes and spiky hair were easy to look at, and no one would guess he spent most of his time sitting behind screens based on his physique. She was pretty sure he probably did yoga or some other strength-building thing while programming.

She opened the door to the living room and found the

trio there, each with a video game controller in their hand and arguing about something on the screen in front of them. It brought a grin to her face. She'd enjoyed many similar evenings while away at school, and it felt a lot like "home." The person nearest her, sitting in a chair by himself while the other two shared a couch, was a dwarf who worked as a dealer at the Dwarven casino, the Underground. The hair on Liam's head was blond and shaggy, pulled into a loose ponytail that mostly failed to restrain it. Three braids made up his beard, adorned with small cylinders of shining silver at the bottom. He wore the same leather vest she'd seen him in during every Zoom call and had large studs in each ear. A constant flow of inventive curses hurtled out of his mouth at the screen, which didn't care, and at his opponents, who found it amusing, to judge by their laughter.

The last person in the room was a Wood Elf who looked far more *Twilight* than Tolkien. Shiannor possessed the ethereal beauty of his species as a baseline that got better from there. His gorgeous bright red hair, which fell in subtle waves to his chest, ensured that he would be noticed by everyone, always. An ornate black tattoo gracefully curved and swept from above his left eye down to his left cheek. His eyelashes had inspired instant envy the first time she'd seen them. *Unfair for his to be longer than mine. Fundamentally unfair.* Ruby was pretty sure that Daphne had designs on him already.

The elf rose to his feet with a victory shout, and both Demetrius and Liam made rude gestures at him. They settled back into their positions with a laugh, and Ruby said, "Hey guys. Room for a fourth?" They turned to her, and each offered a grin. Shiannor threw a controller at her. She sat cross-legged on the floor in front of the screen and looked up to see a choice of race car awaiting her. "*Forza?* Oh, y'all are *so* screwed."

A half-dozen rounds of racing revealed the competitors were more or less evenly matched, which promised good things for the future. They stopped when Daphne arrived bearing pizzas and gathered around the beat-up old rectangular dining room table that had come with the house. They'd rented it fully furnished, and their landlord was a pleasant older Drow Elf woman who managed to be polite most of the time. Which, given Ruby's experience with the seemingly-sarcastic-by-default variety of elves, was a definite bonus. They'd agreed to handle the house's upkeep for a reduction in rent, which pleased all parties involved. Among themselves, they'd decided that by the time they moved out, the house would be much improved as a gift to the building's owner for letting them stay there.

The chairs were mismatched, and none of them seemed to be an original piece of the dining set, if there had been one in the first place. Still, they were comfortable and stable even under the dwarf's mass. Liam had muscles on top of his muscles, which was very apparent given his bare arms. His face looked like it spent a lot of time laughing. The others traded barbs and jokes while Ruby munched on a slice of mushroom and onion pizza and reveled in the relaxed atmosphere. It lasted all of fifteen minutes before the conversation turned to the day's events.

"Did you all hear about what happened at the Mist?" Daphne began.

Shiannor nodded. "Heard some idiots tried to blow the place up and got their asses kicked for it."

Liam snorted in amusement. "The story I got was that they tried to rob the casino. Who does that?"

Ruby sighed. "I can confirm explosions, the robbery, and the ass-kicking. I was there." They all turned to her and asked a jumble of questions, talking over one another. Laughing, they stopped, and Ruby pointed at Demetrius. "Go."

The infomancer pulled a piece of cheese from his lip. "How many were there?"

"Six that I saw."

Liam followed up with, "Was it like an Old West stickup? 'Fill the bags, or I'll fill you full of lead,' that sort of thing?"

She shook her head. "A little less hokey, but yeah, about that."

Daphne frowned. "So the explosions were what, a distraction?"

Ruby nodded. "A nasty one."

The witch's gaze fell to the table. "Yeah. I heard that five people died."

A cold wave washed through Ruby. Intellectually, she'd known the likelihood that the bartender had survived was minimal but had still held out hope in the corner of her mind. To hear that another four people had also fallen victim to the idiotic attempt to rob the casino was brutally emotional. Hot rage replaced the chill inside her, and she had to force herself to remain calm. Such moments risked the maintenance of her illusionary human-ness. The others had started to call her their token Earthling, although they'd spent all or most of their lives on the planet as well.

Shiannor distracted her from her thoughts. "What's really interesting is that I heard it was a civilian who fought off the thieves until the guards could jump in and blast them after the anti-magic stuff had fallen. A civilian with white hair." He gave her a grin that showed his teeth. "I can't help but notice that you fit that description."

Ruby thought about her options, then decided that if there was one group of people she wouldn't keep secrets from—other than her heritage, and maybe not even that, someday—it would be this bunch. Something felt right about them, and she'd had enough friends turn into enemies to know what to watch out for by now. "Yeah, it was me. I have some martial arts training, and they didn't seem like they wanted to shoot the place up, at least at the beginning. I figured they'd underestimate me and I'd be able to make a difference."

Liam crossed his big arms across his chest and nodded in approval. "Apparently you did."

She pushed a strand of hair away from where it had fallen in front of her right eye and reached for another piece of pizza. "I kept them busy until the guards got into the fight, yeah."

Daphne stared at her with a thoughtful expression. "Why? I mean, not why did you get involved, but why did they try to rob a casino?" She shook her head. "Okay, actually, both questions."

Ruby and the others laughed, then she replied, "I got involved because I was afraid they were going to hurt the people inside the cage. For all I knew, the bags they threw in there to fill with cash had bombs in them or something. Plus, I saw some guns." She didn't feel the need to mention that they'd all been carrying at the start because then she'd have to explain away the fact that they'd all dropped their guns simultaneously. "Why did they rob it or blow things up? That I truly don't know. They couldn't have thought they'd get away with it, although at the time they sure *seemed* like they did."

"The first question that detectives in movies always ask is 'who benefits?' So, who would most likely be in a better position today, knowing that the Mist had been attacked?" Demetrius asked.

She shrugged. "Have to list my family on there, I guess. We're the only other Mist Elf casino in town, and anything that hurts the Sunshi family might benefit us. However, I just saw them, and they certainly didn't seem like they'd entered the criminal mastermind business. Frankly, I don't think my brother has the smarts for that role, anyway."

The others chuckled. Shiannor replied, "Could it have been an effort to draw attention to the casino? It's in the news, and that probably won't stay local even on television, much less on the internet. Like they say, 'all publicity is good publicity.'"

Daphne's chair creaked as she leaned back in it and stretched. "Or could be it's something we can't see yet. The start of some sort of action against the casinos? Or against the town? Maybe it's mobsters from Vegas and Reno, and they've had enough of our competition."

Liam threw a cloth napkin and hit her in the face with it. "You've watched too many movies. I'm not buying that idea until DeNiro and Pesci show up and start swearing at me."

Shiannor added, "Don't forget Sharon Stone. She was scorching in that film."

Daphne lifted an eyebrow. "So, you like the older women, do you?"

He grinned. "I wouldn't kick her out of bed. Let's leave it at that."

Ruby focused on the pizza as the conversation devolved from there. In the back of her mind, she kept wondering what the real reason for the casino robbery was—and who was behind it. Because they had a debt to pay, owed to the families of the five people killed because of whatever game they were playing.

CHAPTER SEVEN

The question wouldn't let her stay asleep. She replayed the explosions and the fight repeatedly in her mind and came no closer to understanding the "why" of it all. Ruby considered and discarded theory after theory, from the logical to the ludicrous, and still couldn't reach anything like an answer. She rose as dawn filtered through the pink curtains that adorned the single attic window in her room. With a yawn, she announced, "I need to spruce this place up. Pink is so not happening."

Whoever had lived there previously had possessed a different opinion on the topic. The curtains were pink. The dresser was white with pink accents, and the closet door was a neon version of the shade that almost made her eyes water. She tried not to look at it and wished she knew the right magic to change paint hue. *Cold, heat, force, shadow, illusion, none of those are in the least bit useful against that hideous color.* She couldn't cast any magic that would hide it from her, unfortunately.

They'd all pitched in after the pizza to move the stuff

out of her small U-Haul into the house. The others used magic while she used muscle and grumbled. By the time she'd downed the healing potion to finish off her shoulder and hit the pillows, she'd been achy everywhere, and her desire to let the others know her true nature had increased tenfold. Now, she padded down the stairs to the kitchen, jabbed at the button to brew coffee, failed to hit it and tried more carefully the second time, then took a cold, fast shower to jumpstart her brain. She had things to do; things best started before the tourists got up and out.

She returned to her room and dressed for the day in ripped jeans, heavy black boots, and a white concert t-shirt advertising The Pretty Reckless. People had remarked on her resemblance to the lead singer more than once. She put it down to the hair because she definitely didn't have Taylor Momsen's looks. *Taylor probably can't fight off six guys without getting stomped, either. So, you know, plusses and minuses.* She thought about wearing her leather coat, but the forecast was for heat and more heat, and she would only go so far for fashion. Constant sweating was across that threshold. She pulled the shirt aside to look at her shoulder and nodded in satisfaction. The wound had diminished to only a thin white line that would soon fade. *If not, as Keanu says, chicks dig scars.*

Demetrius was at the dining room table with a huge coffee mug in his hands, and she waved at him as she passed. He grunted something unintelligible that sounded more like good wishes than a curse, so she took it as such.

The house was in an odd little neighborhood, an old one. It dated from before the main part of the town was first fleshed out with businesses, then turned into a tourist destination. Their neighbors were a mix of young and old, the actual structures a blend of old and older. One of them had a feature she prized, a dilapidated detached garage. She walked around behind it to a spot she knew from looking at Google Maps online would be out of sight of the surrounding houses.

She spun in a slow circle to make sure no one was watching and summoned her magic. A veil—essentially an illusion that hid her from sight by replacing her with what someone would see if she wasn't present—spread out from her skin to create a bubble a few inches away. She circled the garage and slipped in through the slight gap permitted by the chain and lock. It turned out to be exactly what she'd hoped—cleanish and deserted. She let the power flow and waved her arms in a wide circle, and a rift appeared in the air. On the opposite side lay a well-lit room, seemingly empty. She strode through, and it immediately transported her from her neighborhood to one of the executive offices in her family's casino, Spirit. They'd designed it as an arrival platform, and a monitor displayed camera angles showing the hallways beyond. When the path cleared, she headed out, took a staircase down to the public level, and stepped onto the three-story escalator that would carry her to the bottom floor.

The Mist emphasized the beauty of nature that the Mist Elves prized. Spirit honored their traditions, their connection to previous generations, and the mysteries of the universe. The decorations were dark in places where sections of the casino looked like stars in the night sky. Others were bright and joyful, like what you felt on a summer day. Overall, the designs tended toward neutrality.

The escalator was in what looked like a mountain that climbed the back of the casino. Vapor occasionally seeped out of the top to suggest active things inside. Real trees carefully cultivated by a small army of workers appeared throughout the gaming floors and the tier of restaurants and shops above them. From her perspective, the way the light fell off as your gaze traveled from the center of the space to the edges was an obvious but effective tactic: a psychological play to make leaving the casino and crossing that boundary seem subtly dangerous. It was both a reference to the idea that one could find spirits at thresholds and a clever business move.

As she stepped off the escalator on the bottom floor, she switched into avoidance mode. The human and nonhuman tourists who frequented the casinos in Magic City tended not to be aware of their surroundings, distracted by the gaming, libations, the scenery, or all of the above. Moving through them without contact was a challenge, and she had no interest in interacting with any of them this morning. She had a purpose, and it lay at the other end of the Ely Strip. She headed for the tram at the back and caught one right before its automatic doors closed. *Next stop, the Mist.*

Other businesses might close after something like the events of the day before. Not a casino, though. Employees, managers, and owners alike wouldn't allow anything short of the act of a vengeful deity to shut them down, and an attempted robbery didn't begin to approach that standard.

They'd cordoned off the areas where the explosions occurred with a velvet rope and metal poles, and workers quietly removed debris and patched up walls and columns. More tourists surrounded the tables and sat in front of the slot machines than she expected. Apparently, they were interested in the event rather than scared by it. *Good for you, unless there's another surprise planned for the Mist. I certainly won't have a drink here again anytime soon.*

She hopped up at intervals to peer over the crowds, searching for her quarry. *I need to get boots with some damn heels on them.* She found them near the casino cage. small yellow numbered markers covered its exterior. Sheriff Alejo stood talking things over with another uniformed officer, not the same one as the day before. Ruby sidled up behind them and waited for a pause in the conversation. As if she had eyes in the back of her head, the woman turned at her arrival. "Miss Achera. Interesting to find you here."

Ruby shrugged. "I don't get blown up every day. I wanted to see this all for myself since I wasn't really capable yesterday." She felt her expression turn down. "Plus, it seems like I owe it to the people who died to at least be here for a minute to remember them."

The other woman tilted her head. "Did you know any of the deceased?"

"No. I haven't even heard their names yet. It still matters." She lifted a hand and let it fall. "I don't know how to say that any better."

Alejo's expression softened a touch. "You don't have to. I get it. Believe me."

Ruby drew a deep breath and exhaled slowly, collecting

herself. "So, have you found anything that makes this make any kind of sense?"

"What do you mean?" Her tone shifted again, and Ruby knew that Alejo was now interrogating her despite the neutral sound of the other woman's voice.

She crossed her arms and gave the officer a level look under lowered eyebrows. "You know exactly what I mean. This was stupid with a capital "S." If they wanted to steal money, this was an idiotic way to do it. If they wanted to knock the place out of business, they didn't do nearly enough to accomplish that. Doesn't make sense."

Alejo matched her posture. "Okay, let's agree it doesn't make sense. What else could it be?"

"You're the expert."

"Not on casinos."

Ruby smiled. "Ah, you're suspicious since my family owns the other Mist Elf place in town."

The sheriff matched her expression almost perfectly. "I wouldn't say suspicious."

She laughed. "Right. Like that's not your default setting. Okay, let's pretend you're neutral. From the perspective of someone involved with casinos, it makes even less sense. It didn't close the place. They simply cordoned off the damage and moved the customers to a different part. They had no chance of making it out with the cash even if they got it out of the cage."

Alejo sighed. "Yeah, that's what I thought, too. Okay, then, why do you think they did it?"

Ruby was well aware that the woman had switched her question back on her. She pulled a thread from the discussion with her roommates. "Publicity, maybe?"

The sheriff laughed darkly. "Kind of a weird way to get attention. More expensive than driving a billboard truck down the street, that's for sure."

"Exactly. As I said, doesn't make sense. On its own, at least."

The other woman's eyes narrowed. "You think this might be part of something bigger?"

Ruby decided to quit trying to spar with her verbally and lay it on the line. "I can't see any reason for it on its own. So logically, it must be part of something else. Or the people who did it were total morons, but they seemed awfully organized and prepared."

Alejo nodded. "You make a lot of sense, and I have to say, my thoughts run in the same direction. Maybe you could sound out your family about it? I don't really have any reason to talk to them, and generally speaking, casino owners aren't the chattiest types unless you have a warrant, a subpoena, or there's been an incident." She gestured around her.

"Information-sharing?"

"Sure. I'll trade you facts on a one-for-one basis, within the bounds of my job."

Ruby shrugged. "Can't ask for more than that. I'll go now and see if I can catch someone at work."

Alejo gave her a piercing look, as if measuring her honesty, then bestowed a final nod upon her. "Sounds good."

She headed for the tram with a sigh, feeling a headache coming on. *Arrived with questions, leaving with responsibilities. I don't know who's behind this nonsense, but they're going to pay. Oh, yes, dire vengeance for inconveniencing me will be mine.*

CHAPTER EIGHT

During the tram ride, her headache not only failed to get better but moved in the opposite direction instead. By the time she disembarked at Spirit, pain radiated throughout her entire head and face, and an ache had developed in her shoulders. She gritted her teeth and concentrated on putting one foot in front of the other, only occasionally banging into other people along her path. Murmured apologies to the blurs she rebounded from were all she could manage.

She made it onto the escalator and kept her balance up to the third floor, which she considered nothing short of a miracle. A college friend had gotten migraines and described one symptom as a narrowing of vision, which made her pretty sure she was experiencing one. The area before her turned into a tunnel, fuzzy at the edges, and even the parts that remained clear seemed to waver.

She made it up the stairs and into the executive offices, waved at the assistant at the desk, and headed for the office in the back. She managed to stay upright until she got there, choked out, "Hi Dad," to the man seated behind the large table in the center of the huge room, and collapsed as her vision first went totally blurry, then completely black.

When she finally climbed the long tunnel that led to consciousness, she was in her bedroom in the family home. She realized it immediately because it was the only place she'd ever had a canopy bed, and since she wasn't outside, those couldn't be clouds over her head. *Good work, Ruby. At least your four-year-old-level logic is still fully functional.* She propped herself up on her elbows, expecting that a wash of pain would accompany the action and pleasantly surprised when it failed to materialize.

She was even more pleased to find Morrigan sitting cross-legged at the bottom of the bed, watching her with a smile. *If she's smiling, I'm probably not going to die. If it were Dralen there with a grin, I'd be less confident.* Plus, she'd hope that if she were on her deathbed, at least one of her two parents, or maybe a healer, might be present. "What's up, munchkin?"

Her sister replied by sticking out her tongue. "If you die, can I have your stuff?"

Ruby gave her the fierce scowl the comment deserved. "No. I demand that it all be buried with me so I can use it in the afterlife."

"Rude." Morrigan tossed her head dramatically. "You should be nice to me, or I'll let the pain-dampening magic

I'm holding fall. Then you'll be all whiny and weepy and probably pass-out-y."

Ruby sat up and lifted her hands. "I surrender. Anything you want of mine is yours, should I no longer be around to use it."

Morrigan grinned. "Good. I'll ask Matthias to draw up a contract."

A laugh escaped Ruby. Then she laughed some more, this time in relief when it didn't hurt. "What the hell happened?"

"You passed out. Mom and Dad said it's not fatal, and I should let them know when you were awake so they could talk to you. I did that when you first opened your eyes, and they'll be up in thirty minutes or so, after their afternoon reading session." The look on her face conveyed her doubtful opinion of that excuse. "I'll stay here and keep you from passing out if you want to take a shower or something."

"You're a good sister, but you're still short."

"Whatever, Casper."

Ruby winced theatrically. "Rude. Nasty. Evil. You have learned well, young Morrigan." Her sister was the only one allowed to call her by the reclaimed insult, and she sketched a slight bow as Ruby passed on the way to the shower.

Instead of waiting, Ruby found her way down to the study where her parents awaited her, seated in two of the four leather wingback chairs that faced each other over a low table. A teapot sat in the center, and she immediately recognized the scent of the herbal brew used to fortify magic. It didn't do a whole lot, but every bit of energy she could add to her stockpile was welcome due to the constant expenditure required to maintain her disguise. *That's one of the first things I'm going to make once I get the lab set up, some sort of illusion power repository.* She pushed that idea back into the mental file cabinet with her other future projects and sat across from them.

The room had two large windows on the wall opposite her, and leather furniture, tapestries on the walls, tables big enough to hold the complicated board games they all loved to play, and other creature comforts outfitted the rest. Of the entire house, it was the space that felt the most lived-in, the one she most associated with being *home*, other than her bedroom.

She lifted the heavy mug to her lips and took a deep drink. "Sorry for the drama."

Her father laughed. "It'll be the talk of the casino for days, I'm sure."

Ruby winced. "Nikolas saw?"

He nodded. "You know what a gossip he is. By now, the entire place has heard about it."

"Excellent. So, I'd kind of expected that if I woke up at all, I'd be in the hospital, or at the healer's, or something. What's the deal?"

Her mother grinned. "You've been given an amazing gift, Ruby."

She barked a laugh. "Migraines? I don't think 'gift' is the word I'd use. Probably more like 'curse.' Or 'affliction.'"

Her father lifted an eyebrow. "Or perhaps due punishment? Karma's a bitch, as they say. I'm sure you weren't a saint while you were away at college. Maybe fate is balancing the scales."

Sinnia swept out a long arm to slap her husband's shoulder with the back of her hand. "Hush, Rayar. This is no time for stupid jokes." She met Ruby's eyes. "You're being called."

"Well, whoever it is could have used the phone. Knocking me out wasn't required." She sighed at the end of the automatic sarcasm. "How do you mean? By who? To do what?"

Her father replied, "By Oriceran. To return and undertake your *venamisha*."

She blinked, stunned. "Wait. What?"

Her mother nodded. "You're the right age, and the symptoms you exhibit are the appropriate ones."

The historical tales of the Mist Elves included many stories of the *venamisha*. It took different forms and meant different things, depending on the story, but it was always a trip or a quest of some kind that led the person undertaking it both inward and outward. The closest analogue she'd seen in Earth literature was a vision quest or spirit quest, but neither of those encompassed the whole of it. It was like those, plus a pilgrimage, plus a death curse, all in one. "So what you're saying is that I either go back to Oriceran, or the thing in my head will eventually kill me."

They nodded, and her mother replied, "That's how the *venamisha* works."

"Have either of you ever done one?" It hadn't ever occurred to her to ask them. She'd never known someone who was called or heard of anyone outside the stories who'd had the experience.

Both shook their heads in reply. Her father added, "The last confirmed calling was more than a century ago, but of course, there's no way to be sure. One of the mystics might have been called but not shared it." That secretive group of Mist Elves was most appropriately compared to monks on Earth, from what she knew, although she'd never visited their home or spoken to one of them.

"Okay. So, no options is what you're saying. As I remember, it's something I must do alone because anything else would be far less dramatic and story-worthy." She pushed down the sarcasm with an effort. "So, do I have to do it with a headache trying to knock me out the whole time?"

Her mother answered, "No, the pain will go away once you're back on Oriceran, for a while at least. Long enough for you to do whatever you're being called to do."

"But we don't know what that is."

A shrug from her father. "The stories say it's always personal to the one called. You can probably be reasonably sure that nothing you've read about will happen again, but beyond that, it's supposed to be unique."

Ruby closed her eyes and finished her tea, then leaned her head into the corner of the chair's tall back. The cool leather felt good. "Okay, well, you should probably be aware I've promised Morrigan she can have all my stuff if I don't survive."

They laughed, and her mother commented, "That child is trouble."

Her father added, "No more than Ruby was at her age." He pointed at her. "Certainly not more than you are now."

She frowned. "I am *not* trouble. I just seem to attract more excitement than my share." Actually, she felt decidedly troublesome and decided that maybe more than one revelation might be on the table. "So, have we hidden my heritage all this time because of something to do with the *venamisha?*"

Her father frowned at her mother, then shook his head. "It is perhaps related, but not a case of cause and effect. We know that you're troubled by not knowing." He chuckled softly. "I don't suppose you'd believe that we're magically unable to talk about it, would you?"

Ruby shook her head. "No, afraid not."

Her mother said, "Please bear with us for a little longer. Once you've completed the *venamisha*, perhaps we can reveal it. Know that it's for your good."

"Uh-huh. Just like always. Okay, you've got a deal. I'll chill out about it for a while. But not for a *long* while, if you get my drift." She sighed, then remembered her earlier conversation. "Hey, I was coming to see you for a reason. I spoke with Sheriff Alejo, and she wondered if you might have any insight into why someone would do what they did at the Mist."

Sinnia looked thoughtful. "So, she thinks it wasn't simply a robbery?"

"Nope. That doesn't make sense. They couldn't have hoped to get away with it."

Rayar nodded slowly, his fingers steepled and resting lightly on his chin. "So, first possibility, if the Sunshis are behind it, it might point to insurance fraud or an effort to get their names in the news. Still, there are a lot of other, better ways to accomplish both those things. Second possibility, it truly was random, but I agree that seems unlikely. Which leaves the third possibility as the most likely: that this is part of something bigger."

Ruby nodded. "That's my conclusion, too. I think the sheriff's as well."

He straightened in his chair. "I can't imagine it's one of the council members." The casino owners all also held positions on the council that oversaw both the city and the kemana. "That means it's probably an outsider."

"Human organized crime?"

Her father shrugged. "Maybe. Or perhaps other magicals with an agenda. Might be working with someone local, I suppose. We'll have to discuss this and possibly increase our security in all the casinos in response."

Sinnia ventured, "Could that have been the objective? Cause a need for more security?"

Ruby nodded. "Seems possible. That might result in strangers with expanded access in our places."

Rayar replied, "Well, all we can do is what we can do. Add floor security with minimal access, move our trusted staff to expanded access. I'll talk it over with the others. Fortunately, there's a bunch of private security companies that have been looking for additional work. It shouldn't be a problem to find people."

Her mother beamed at her. "We'll have it all figured out by the time you get back. No time like the present to find out what your *venamisha* has in store for you." She almost vibrated with excitement. "My daughter, *called*. Who would have thought it?"

Ruby sighed. "Well, given that it's literally life or death, I guess I better get underway since I'd at least slightly prefer the former to the latter." She consoled herself with the amusing fact that if her mother wanted to continue to maintain the secret of Ruby's heritage, she wouldn't be able to tell anyone about the calling. *Heh. She's gonna be ticked to high heaven when she realizes that.*

CHAPTER NINE

Ruby stepped through the portal that connected her bedroom to her family's home on Oriceran. The pain that had begun to creep back into her head vanished as if crossing the threshold between planets had scraped it away. A wave of her hand dispelled the opening, and she stretched and yawned, feeling the relief of being completely without a headache since the moment it had started at the Mist. Her sister's efforts had dulled the ache but not banished it, she now realized. Being free of it was pure pleasure.

Her landing spot was her bedroom, and she moved immediately into the ritual she always used when coming to the magical planet. She visited at least weekly, sometimes more than that, for training with her Mist Elf mentor Keshalla, a woman whose prowess in hand-to-hand fighting was second only to her ability to perform combat magic. A tall wardrobe on the far wall held what Ruby thought of as her Elf clothes, and she quickly changed.

Brown leather pants worn often enough to be soft and supple tucked into knee-high matching boots with laces to hold them in place. A wide leather belt secured a half-sleeved undertunic in black. Metal-ringed holes in two rows throughout its length adorned that item, and she attached a couple of pouches to the back and a pair of sheaths to the sides. Within the latter rested knives with slightly curved blades positioned for a cross-draw. Her overtunic was sleeveless and tight, with laces down the front. It had thin metal strips running through it to protect her from impact and was the brilliant blue of her house, with a silver stripe down each side.

The final element was the sword, the weapon she currently studied. Her Mist Elf mentor had already taught her knives, throwing knives, darts, sticks, and bladed sticks. The single sword was the next-to-last traditional weapon she would learn, and when she'd mastered it, she'd move on to paired swords. She was already training to use the sword and a knife together, in addition to her instruction with the larger blade on its own.

She positioned the sword's sheath over her back. The holder featured a slit that would allow her to draw the weapon from it cleanly. The pommel stuck up over her shoulder, a warning to anyone who saw it of her martial accomplishment. Only those with the proper training were entitled to display such weapons openly, and any who chose to violate that convention often found themselves tested by others who had earned the right.

Her penultimate task was to pull her hair back into a hasty warrior's knot, held in place by a pair of thin metal rods. Finally, she let go of the constant thread of magic that powered her disguise, revealing her pointed ears. When she used her power, the tattoos on her bare arms would appear, and in truth, she loved the sight of them. If not for her parents' desires, she'd flaunt them all the time. *Maybe one day. For now, I guess I need to go figure out where I'm being summoned to.*

She didn't have a better plan than seeking out Keshalla and asking her. The woman was unique among the Mist Elves Ruby had met, more mystical than most but more martial than any mystic. She'd been very lucky to be chosen as her student since her mentor accepted only one at a time. Training when together was only part of Ruby's obligations. She was expected to continue on her own while on Earth and had done so diligently, both in magic and melee. Disappointing her teacher was *not* something a smart person did.

She stepped out of the house into the small village, one of many loosely affiliated groupings of Mist Elves that resided in the mountains. They only ever called them "the mountains," not caring if others existed beyond their lands. They lived high up but had plateaus for farming, forests for game, and rivers for fish and water. The higher one climbed, the less integrated the village was with the rest. The mystics occupied the highest part of the pinnacle, literally living in the mist for substantial portions of the year.

This particular spot was about two-thirds of the way up, still low enough to desire interaction with others, but high enough that its residents possessed a keen sense of individualism. Both those qualities had led the two oldest families in the village to create the Mist Elf foothold on

Earth, and most of the rest who had come over to join them on the other planet had been from lower elevations.

Keshalla had received a formal invitation to live in MountHaven, of course, but was decidedly unlikely to accept it. By her declaration, she was uninterested in Earth since she still had so much to learn and experience on Oriceran. The idea of the other woman standing on the Ely Strip was so ridiculous that Ruby couldn't picture it.

Five other homes created a rough oval on the plateau. Low grass covered the center area, but it was otherwise empty except for boulders that no one had ever moved, sitting here and there on the central lawn. The time difference meant that it was barely past noon here although it would be well into Magic City's evening. She took several steps toward the middle, her hands on her knife hilts as she looked around suspiciously. Fewer people than she'd expected were in evidence. One figure darted away at the edge of her vision, a child to judge by the laughter. *At least someone's enjoying themselves.* She checked the sun's position to confirm that she was at the right place at the right time. *Where is everyone? More importantly, where is Keshalla?*

Both questions received answers as a tall woman stepped into view on the grassy field's opposite side. She was dressed as Ruby was, but in crimson and black, the colors of fire and soil. Her hair was inky, a rarity among the Mist Elves, offering a high contrast to her pale skin. She carried a frankly astonishing number of weapons strapped to her clothes, and two pommels stuck up over her shoulders. She called, "Welcome back, *minari*. It is a momentous day."

Ruby nodded and slowly advanced toward her,

knowing where this was headed. "Indeed, *shenai*. Are you prepared to guide me on the path of my calling?" Faces peered out of windows in the houses around, watching but also providing them a measure of privacy.

She spread her arms wide. "Such a service must be earned, young one."

Ruby's lips curved in a smile. "I wouldn't want to damage you, ancient one."

The other woman's laugh was like the joyful chime of a bell. "Do your best. Manage a hit, and I will give you a clue to lead you where you wish to go immediately. Fail, and you train first until the sun goes down."

Ruby gave a dramatic sigh, having expected something like this the moment she knew she'd have to ask the other woman for help. It was test after test with her, or maybe one long one that marked their relationship's boundaries. "Must we?"

Her mentor lifted a hand, palm up, then curved the fingers inward in an invitation. "We must."

Ruby charged, drawing her sword from over her shoulder as she ran. A thin sheath of force flowed from her hand down the weapon and covered its sharp edge. It would still hurt if it connected but wouldn't cut or pierce. That was as safe as her mentor would permit, now that she had achieved, in her words, "A barely adequate level of proficiency."

Keshalla opted for her knives, unsheathing them in a cross-draw and spinning them once as she shifted into a battle stance: left leg forward, body pivoted perpendicular to Ruby's line of approach, knees bent, front dagger guarding high, rear one positioned over her stomach. It was a balanced position from which her teacher could defend or attack without giving a hint of her intention before she started to move.

Ruby's preferred tactic in such a situation would be a fast pass to her opponent's backhand, spinning as she arrived to whip her sword around in a horizontal blow. It would force the other woman to at least turn, which might break her balance enough for a follow-up. The problem was that Keshalla had taught her that approach, so she'd expect it. She could use illusion against an opponent who wasn't a Mist Elf, as she had with the men in the casino, but her mentor would be ready for that, too. *So, let's try something a little more brazen.*

She waved her free hand in a fast arc, dispatching a line of force magic at her foe's feet. Despite the invisible nature of the power, Keshalla skipped over it with ease. While she was in the air, Ruby smashed directly into the older Mist Elf, sent her tumbling backward, and continued her rush. Her sword slashed down at the other woman's head.

Ruby saw the grin on her teacher's face for an instant before the magic-assisted roll that brought her back to her feet hid it. Keshalla used magic as naturally as breathing, subtly increasing her speed and strength with minimal bursts of power. It caused Ruby's strike to miss, and she barely managed to slip a force shield in the way of the sidekick that slammed into her and sent her flying sideways. While the magical barrier stole a lot of the blow's power, it didn't invalidate the laws of physics. It would have taken a much stronger and layered shield to absorb all the kinetic energy transferred during the attack. It simply spread the impact over a larger space and prevented broken ribs but failed to keep her from moving.

A well-angled force blast against the ground got her upright in time for her feet to land on the dirt. She skidded backward, focusing on keeping her balance and completely aware that the other woman was charging in, the naked metal in her fists glinting in the sunlight. Ruby let her eyes go soft and made sure she kept Keshalla's entire body in view. A front kick led the way, and she moved aside in a smooth step to avoid it, knowing it was almost certainly a feint. The looping overhand stab at her head with the back knife wasn't the real danger either, although it required her to shift the sword slightly to deflect it, lifting the weapon to meet the blow. That opened her for the primary threat, the left-hand knife jabbing in at her seemingly unprotected stomach.

She twisted away in case the force shield she'd wrapped around the target area wouldn't be sufficient. The feel of Keshalla's magic peeling hers away to give the blade access confirmed the wisdom of that choice. It scraped across the metal in her clothing and failed to penetrate. She reversed the pivot and leapt, rotating her back knee across her body in a blurred strike at the other woman's chest. Keshalla effortlessly danced aside. One moment she was there, and the blow was about to connect. The next she wasn't, and worse, Ruby had lost sight of her.

Not because of the speed of her movement, but because of the shadow magic the other woman had dropped over Ruby's head like a hood. It took only a half-second to marshal her power to blast it away. She dove forward and to the right as she did, toward the open space she'd seen before everything went dark. Her shoulder roll brought her smoothly up to her feet. She kept running in that direction but whipped the sword around her back, pommel high and blade down. It intercepted one knife with a satisfying *clank*, but the other thrown weapon slammed into her back. The magic her teacher had infused it with made it hit like a bag of bricks, and Ruby went down into the dirt.

She was already scrambling up, ready for more, but Keshalla called, "Enough." The victor held out her palms, the blades leapt into them, and she slid them back into their sheaths. "So. Time to train. Your calling can wait until tomorrow."

Ruby nodded. "As you say, *shenai*."

A broad grin spread across the other woman's face. "As it should be, *minari*."

CHAPTER TEN

Their training had been long and intensive, and when it ended Ruby had spent another hour discussing the calling with Keshalla. The older Mist Elf knew more stories about those who had undertaken the *venamisha*, but it still wasn't much to go on in the end. Each person's experience appeared to be different, with no consistency in the tales except for an undercurrent of warning. Some never returned, and some returned broken. Of those who had claimed success, some had access to previously unheard of magics and became teachers, increasing the knowledge and abilities of the Mist Elves.

Others rejoined society with grand ideas that had changed the course of Mist Elf history. The first mystic had only become so after her journey. Ruby thought that she'd probably enjoy being a mystic—for maybe a year, year and a half tops—and only if she came back with some marvelous brewing knowledge and created an Oriceran craft brewery, like the Benedictine monastery on the outskirts of Magic City. *It seems unlikely that I would get some kind of spiritual calling that will kill me if I don't obey merely to create the world's most wonderful stout.*

Keshalla had shaken her head and clucked her tongue at Ruby's preparations. "You're not going on vacation, girl," she'd chastised, then portaled them both to her home farther up the mountain. Her mentor had no neighbors and chose a solitary life except for her teaching and occasional good deeds toward the other Mist Elves living nearby. However, the armory in her house would have put a castle to shame. Blades and bows covered three of the four walls, from punch daggers and pistol crossbows to two-handed swords that she'd need magic to lift and longbows that were at least as tall as her. The last wall held shelves and cabinets, and it was to those her teacher had gone to retrieve the things she felt Ruby couldn't do without.

Now, after a solid night's sleep, Ruby was ready. She had everything from the previous day, plus a good deal more. A sheath strapped to each calf held a throwing knife. Keshalla had informed her that she'd need to have new boots made to accommodate the blades in the future. A fine chain shirt now rested between her under- and over- tunics, providing additional protection against edged weapons. A pouch on her lower back's right side contained two potions in metal flasks, one healing and one energy. One on her left side's lower back held travel rations, dense food bars that could keep her going for days. The outside of each thigh had a metal canteen full of water attached to it. Finally, the older woman had given her an ebony amulet on a matching chain that rested around her neck. The proper command, *"kagji,"* would create a powerful shield to protect her without drawing upon her magic.

Ruby was as ready as she could be. She repeated the step out of her house's front door from the day before. The sun was rising over the horizon, and everything was still and serene. A deep inhalation followed by a slow exhalation centered her for the adventure ahead, and as she closed her eyes, she opened herself to the magic spinning around her as Keshalla had instructed. It was a matter of letting her internal barriers open a touch so her power could taste the currents flowing in the planet's very air. She sensed the calling and instinctively knew which way to go. *Damn it. Of course.* She turned in the proper direction, and when she opened her eyes again, they confirmed her expectation. *Up the mountain. Why isn't it ever* down *the mountain? Or "Go to the nearest Starbucks?" That'd be nice.* She growled, "All right, Ruby, quit whining and start moving," then obeyed her orders.

———

The climb hadn't been particularly arduous, but Ruby felt it in her legs by the time she reached the spot where the ambient magic directed her to leave the path and head out onto a small plateau on the right-hand side. It led about thirty feet to the edge, and she looked down to see a drop of several hundred feet. Beside her, a thin but consistent trickle of water dropped to splash into a small lake below. *Probably not deep enough to save me if I fell, so maybe I'll back up a little.* Heights weren't a problem for her, but there was no point being unnecessarily reckless. *Only a necessary amount of recklessness is required*, she thought in Keshalla's voice and laughed.

Out loud, she said, "Okay, then, what's the deal? I'm here. Hello?" No response was forthcoming, and she opened her inner barriers a little more. A faint sense of *something* came from the mountain, and she followed the water's path as it curved back toward the stone wall. The rivulet wasn't deeper than her foot, nor wider than it, where it emerged from the rock. Still, something was definitely back there, a presence or a summons, maybe. Clearly, she had to get through the barrier in front of her.

Ruby explored the area with her magical senses, opening the inner barriers even more, and received only the same confirmation that a mystery lay behind the rock wall before her. She walked the length of it, trailing her hands along it in case an illusion compromised her vision, but found nothing. She sighed and called, "Really? I thought you'd be more subtle." Doubtless she imagined the low laughter that seemed to echo through the wind rippling across the plateau. "Fine, then. Have it your way."

She returned to the spot where the water emerged from the stone. It was a rough triangular hole, with a crack running several inches upward from the apex. The simplest solution would be to blast the area with force magic until whatever was weakest broke away, but the possibility it would be the ground under her feet that failed first argued against that plan. She found a couple of rocks of the right size in the stream bed and made sure they were wet before jamming them tightly into the small vertical crevice. Then she backed up, created a narrow wall of force in front of her in case, and summoned flame to an upraised palm. She directed it in a thin line into the rocks she'd chosen, causing them to heat up rapidly. The water turned to steam, providing extra pressure, and the crack grew bigger with a loud *snap*. Shrapnel bounced off the magical barrier that protected her.

She nodded in satisfaction and repeated the process several times until enough room existed that she could crawl through without taking a bath while doing so. She packed flames into a ball of force and rolled it into the opening, revealing a tunnel beyond it that she would also have to crawl through. A force push sent it rolling further to show a larger area, although she couldn't make out anything other than its existence from where she was. *Okay, then, ready or not, here I come.* She wrapped herself in a force shield that extended an inch from her body to avoid getting dirty, muddy, or otherwise injured and crawled through the low tunnel.

The cavern it emptied into required a jump down of a few feet to reach the floor. Overhead, the ceiling soared two or three stories high, and purple crystals ranging from small to immense adorned the irregular surface. The largest was probably twice the size of a Mustang, her current wish-list car. *Not that I need a car as such, but it sure would be nice to drive around with the top down and past Jennifer's house once a day.* She chuckled at her pettiness, summoned more force-and-flame lights, and rolled them in different directions. The walls and floor had been shaped by muscle or magic into smooth surfaces carved with a repeating geometric pattern that made her eyes hurt if she stared at it too long. Only one exit led from the room, and only one object was visible inside it: a huge brazier in the center, hanging by a trio of golden chains from a pyramid of thick black metal poles. It shone in the flickering fire from her globes, the highlights enhancing the polished silver of the bowl.

Ruby walked around it, looking for clues, but none came. She reversed her path, shifting her gaze outward, but saw nothing of interest other than the tunnel she'd entered through. "Well, if this is your idea of a warm reception, you have to work on your social skills." Her voice echoed strangely in the room, as though it bounced off more surfaces than were apparent to the eye. She shrugged. "Fine, be that way." She created a ball of fire in her palm and tossed it into the bowl.

The brazier surged to life. A wash of flame leapt up over the chains and supports and almost reached the ceiling. The fire spread along the floor from under the object. It filled in the geometric patterns in unpredictable ways, ignoring some and jumping across gaps to others with no understandable reason. She stepped nimbly around the expanding fire, ready to bolt back for the doorway. Her magic told her this was real flame, not an illusion, and she had no desire to be cooked in the mystical pizza oven that the room might become.

When the fire finished filling in new spaces, a low rumbling sounded across from where she'd entered. A piece of the wall descended into the floor to reveal another tunnel beyond, again crafted by magic or muscle. She muttered, "Come into my parlor, said the spider to the fly," and paused to consider her options. *Okay, I have no options other than to ignore the calling and apparently die or keep going. Guess I'll keep going.* With a headshake at the bizarre life she led, she headed for the door out of the room. "I don't know who's behind this, or if you're listening, but I'm going to slap you so many times when this is over, you'll be unconscious for a week."

Her internal voice observed, "Assuming you survive, of course."

Shut it. If I die, at least I won't have to listen to you anymore, which will be a gods-damned bonus if you ask me.

Laughter echoed in her ears as she crossed into the tunnel.

CHAPTER ELEVEN

This passage proved to be far longer than the previous one had been, seeming to descend into the mountain. Ruby was thankful that she didn't have to crawl but more than a little daunted at the notion that she might have to make the trip in reverse once she finished whatever she was here to do.

The tales she'd heard of the *venamisha* hadn't mentioned going into the mountain, although several had included climbing it. Others had described stepping through portals although as far as she knew, those people could have also wound up right where she was. None of the stories had been anything like highly detailed, as if those who had undertaken the journey had been unwilling —or unable since it involved magic—to remember or share particulars. The air felt generally dry but not dusty. It seemed as if the occupants had left only weeks before although to her knowledge no one had lived inside the mountain in forever.

Literally forever since the Mist Elves had no records of anyone ever making their home within the massive tower of rock that was the dominant feature of their geography. So, it seemed even stranger that the well-kept passage remained that way, given the lack of inhabitants.

The voice in her head observed, "You're babbling because you're nervous."

Shut it. I'm not babbling, and I'm not nervous. Scared out of my wits, maybe, but not nervous. In truth, a mix of fear and anticipation filled her, and each step forward felt more and more like she was moving toward where she was supposed to be. As someone who lived most of her life under a disguise, that feeling was decidedly rare. *I hope I'm able to tell people about this once it's over.*

It led into complete darkness and required Ruby to summon another orb of flame and force to light her way. She made this one bigger, about the size of a soccer ball, and kicked it forward, picturing imaginary teammates to pass it to. That entertained her for five minutes, was a neutral experience for the next five, and had become downright annoying by the time a quarter-hour had passed. Then a glow emanated from the path ahead, and a ninety-degree turn revealed the entrance to a room. "Thank the gods." She dispelled the orb and stepped carefully onto the chamber's carved floor, staying on the outermost oval of tiles.

Etched squares, rectangles, and trapezoids covered every surface, each with a design that seemed to have nothing to do with the ones around it. Some glowed, again seemingly at random, and filled the room with light. The anarchy that met her eyes put her on edge, and she focused instead on the four tall columns set in a diamond shape in the space. "Probably perfectly symmetrical. Who or whatever designed this place loved geometry." The cylinders were at different heights, the shortest ending about ten feet above the floor, the tallest reaching twenty or more. The ceiling stood another twenty above that.

Ruby crouched with a frown. *The pillars probably have something to do with how I get out of here, but there must be more to it.* She summoned a ball of force and threw it at the nearest column. It bounced off with no effect, but when it hit the floor, the tile it landed on vanished, and the sphere fell through. *Okay, then. Parkour challenge with something nasty under the floor. Awesome.*

Her inner voice offered, "Probably bottomless. Or spikes, maybe. Poisoned spikes. With barbs. Several barbs."

You're not helping. Other people used the phrase "My own worst enemy" metaphorically. She was convinced her brain actively sought her destruction most of the time. Out loud, she said, "Okay, then. Let's do this." She reached over her shoulder to check that her sword was secure in its scabbard and used a force blast to propel herself into the air, aiming at the lowest pillar, which was also the nearest. As she arrived at the top of her arc, a shimmer to the side gave her enough warning to summon a force buckler to her left arm. A wicked-looking dart, complete with sharp barbs along its length, struck it and dropped to the floor. She landed awkwardly and fell to her stomach, grabbing the lip of the column to keep herself from rolling off.

Another shimmer appeared, this one at the top of the highest pillar, set across the room from her. When it faded, it revealed an elderly Mist Elf with her hands clasped before her. The woman wore a long pale blue robe that set off her almost translucently white skin. Thin braids of ivory hair fell over her shoulders and reached to her waist. Her eyes matched the robe. She nodded. "Welcome, *junra*."

Ruby had heard that word only once or twice before in relation to the mystics. It meant something like "pilgrim." She offered a small bow appropriate to the woman's apparent age. "Thank you, grandmother." All elderly women were called grandmother. It was a thing the Mist Elves did.

A smile creased the other woman's face. "Polite. That's good, that's good. Also smart enough not to walk along the floor. A promising sign."

"Again, thank you." Another small bow. She'd had manners drilled into her by both her family and Keshalla. *Then again, etiquette can only take one so far.* "So, what's the deal here?" She gestured around the room. "I don't see an exit other than the one I entered through."

The room's other occupant nodded. "A challenge, as I'm sure you expected from the outset. Good luck, *junra*. I offer you this word of advice." Her smile widened. "Don't fall."

She vanished in the now-familiar shimmer, which replicated on the other pedestals. When it ended, the tallest column was empty, but people inhabited the other two. To her left was a leather armor-clad Mist Elf gripping a drawn bow. To her right, a matching figure with fire already coalescing in his palm. *Well, that escalated quickly.* She called up a force shield on each arm and deflected the attacks, congratulating herself mentally on not overreacting and jumping to attack. That warm feeling lasted all of five seconds before the column beneath her trembled. Panicked, she kept up the shield against the fireballs and dropped the other while launching herself across the room to the tall pillar on a burst of force magic.

She landed and spun to find the others had moved as well. Now the caster was on her right and the archer directly opposite her. Her only ranged weapons were her throwing knives, and she felt none too confident about making the toss across the distance that separated them. *Magic it is.* Ruby delegated part of her attention, the one controlling the shield on her right arm, to the foe that now hurled alternating balls of fire and electricity at her. Her defense was adequate but maintaining it was slowly draining her energy. She threw her left arm forward, palm out, and channeled a burst of force from it directly at the archer's face. It intercepted a pair of arrows, shattered them, and missed the target when her enemy crouched. She growled and lowered her aim, sending another at his torso that he jumped to avoid. When he landed, he took to the air again immediately, this time toward the empty pillar on her left. The one on her right jumped as well, to the one his partner had vacated. She copied the motion, descending a level to the platform on that side. She called, "Quite a dance we have here."

They didn't reply, only resumed their attacks. *Okay, be that way.* Given the archer's nimble grace, there was only one good option. She shot a wide cone of electricity at him and maintained her shield against the other. Her foe tried to jump out of the way, but she'd anticipated the move and shifted the cone with him. It caught him in mid-transit, and his body stiffened and fell. While she was distracted by the overwhelming desire to see what happened when he hit, the caster smashed her legs with a burst of force and knocked them out from beneath her. She scrabbled at the surface of the platform as she slid off and managed to grab the edge with one hand.

Ruby hung for the moment it took to realize she'd survived, then created a force platform to stand on, attached to the pillar. It shook violently as if the structure was trying to throw her off, but it was enough. She launched herself off it with another magical blast and leapt. The caster tried her tactic against her, but he'd chosen poorly, assuming she'd go to one of the empty columns. He couldn't redirect the attack fast enough to catch her as she hurtled toward him. She dispatched quick bursts of ice, his preference for fire suggesting that maybe he'd dislike its opposite. The caster intercepted them with a flame shield, and she called up one of ice an instant before she hit.

Her momentum propelled him to the platform's edge, where he windmilled for a perilous second before he smiled at her and fell over the edge. She turned, her shield at the ready, but no other opponents appeared. Only an exit from the room, directly opposite the one she'd come in. *Well, it was too much to hope it would be only one challenge, right?*

CHAPTER TWELVE

The tunnel beyond the door continued to wind down into the mountain. The entertainment of kicking her light ahead had faded within the first five minutes this time. Still, Ruby didn't want to expend any more magic to move it differently, fearing she'd need all of it before the *venamisha* was complete. She'd tweaked a muscle during one of the jumps that hadn't announced itself until the adrenaline had worn off, and the unexpected twinges when she moved the wrong way made her grumpy. She barked, "You know, I didn't train in engineering for six years to wind up as a damned mountain... walking... person. Whatever they're called." She kicked the ball harder and almost got hit in the face as it bounced off a turn she hadn't seen ten feet ahead.

She retrieved the errant item and carried it around the corner. Another opening into another room, but darkness beyond. A roll sent the ball forward, revealing a tiled floor similar to the previous one. Where those patterns had been geometric, these flowed, connecting from block to block.

The ball stopped moving, showing nothing but an empty floor. Remembering the brazier in the first room, Ruby directed a thin line of flame at the nearest block, but nothing happened. She tried ice and electricity with similar results. With a scowl, she observed, "You know, force doesn't make sense, and shadow is, well, dark." However, a bolt of the latter activated the runes, which glowed purple as they filled in around the room and illuminated it from the nearer side to the opposite end.

Stone platforms hung in mid-air, their thick smoothed edges glowing with the purple lines. The seven surfaces were positioned at different heights and looked too far apart to jump from one to the next, even if they were on the same level. They climbed toward the center of the room, then descended again on the far side. She used a force blast to fly up to the nearest, roughly eight feet off the floor on her left. She advanced unhindered to the one before the centermost, and the center platform shimmered at her arrival nearby. When the glow faded, an elderly man, almost the twin of the woman from the previous room, nodded at her. "Welcome, *junra*."

She sketched a bow, holding it for the requisite amount of time plus a couple of seconds. "Thank you, grandfather. Please tell me we don't have to do battle with one another."

He laughed at the jest, seeming entirely gleeful. "Fortunately not, as I likely couldn't have defeated you in my prime, which passed so long ago I can scarcely remember it. No, your challenge here is of a different kind."

"Do tell," Ruby replied, and he laughed again.

"When you ascend to this platform, you will be unable to advance or retreat without overcoming the obstacles on the others. The ones behind you will be easier; the ones ahead, more difficult and more dangerous. You may, of course, turn back now, before invoking this next stage of the *venamisha*."

Yeah, right. Like Keshalla would ever let me hear the end of that. "Once I've done so, it's over?" He laughed and faded into another shimmer without speaking again. She shouted, "I'll take that as a yes! Done deal!" Before she could overthink it, she launched herself into the air and landed on the center platform. The room around her platform fell into darkness, then the two nearest it illuminated. A shriek filled the air as lightning crashed down on the one before her, transforming into a cylinder made of that power that extended ten feet toward the ceiling. She turned to look at the one behind, which flames covered. *Ice would take care of that one. Electricity, that's more difficult.* She considered flying into the darkness and trusting her memory to where the next one in the sequence was but quickly abandoned the idea. *They'd prevent that, I'm sure.*

The logical option would be to encase it in force, but the continued sparking and snapping meant that it would be a constant drain to maintain against the lightning while she dealt with the next challenge. *So, I need to figure out how to limit that. I have just the thing.* She unhooked the canteen from her right thigh, dumped out the tiny amount of liquid that remained, then threw the cap at the platform. It deflected from the outside of the magical cylinder. "Okay, then, how about this?" With careful deliberation, she used pulses of force magic to lift it over the field and drop it on the platform from high above. It attracted the lightning to it, and she quickly created a double force barrier above it to insulate herself from the metal, then launched herself over.

The next one illuminated. On it stood a statue with its arms extended like it wanted to hug her. Circular holes were positioned where its face, hands, and heart would be. Magic filled each, cycling through ice and fire in quick succession. She put her hands on her hips and observed to the room, "This looks way too easy." A flick of her fingers sent a bolt of flame into the ice, and the figure's forearm shattered. A moan echoed through the space, and the statue moved with a groaning scrape, pulling the arm in protectively. Ruby frowned. "Okay, what the hell is this? I have to face the challenge, but get a guilt trip too?" She focused her will, ready to strike all the remaining spots simultaneously so she wouldn't have to watch the figure suffer, but stopped before doing so. *As a test of magic, this is neither difficult nor dangerous. So it must be something else.* "Oh, I hope I'm right about this." She checked the draw on her daggers, wrapped herself in a force shield, and blasted toward the apparent target dummy.

The circles disappeared when she landed beside the statue, and it smiled at her before it, too, vanished. The next one lit up, revealing a beautiful pair of swords on a stand. They were pristine, even from a distance. Once beside them, it became clear that they were magical, each faintly glowing in a cascade of changing colors. A double sheath sat beside them, and she knelt to take it up, almost overwhelmed with desire for the blades, which she was certain would render any further encounter trivial.

Almost overwhelmed. Her internal voice cautioned,

"Hold up there a second, grabby. This is still supposed to be a challenge, right, not a reward?"

Ruby frowned, but her hands stopped before they touched the weapons, despite the gravitational pull of her need for them. *You're right. The truth is, I haven't earned the right to wear these yet.* She stood, and with a regret that felt almost like breaking, said, "I will not accept these. Still, if you could keep them around until I'm ready, I'd appreciate it."

The weapons vanished, the lights came back to full intensity, and the exit appeared. Internal Ruby asked, "What would you do without me?"

Be a lot happier, probably. For that one, thanks. She paused to drink from her remaining canteen and refocus her mind, then launched herself through the doorway.

CHAPTER THIRTEEN

The tunnel came to an abrupt end as the path suddenly leveled and opened into a chamber she hadn't seen coming because of the angle. It was similar to the room above in that the walls and floor were crafted and covered with geometrical symbols. It was dissimilar to it by virtue of the statues positioned all around the perimeter and the fact that it was easily three times as large. *Maybe a little bigger than two basketball courts side by side, but rounded,* her brain supplied helpfully.

The brazier in the center was proportionate to the one in the larger room, and she hurled a ball of fire into it before she could second-guess the wisdom of doing so. Again the fire spread, but this time in straight lines to each of the statues, where it vanished only to reappear in several of the figures' cupped hands. When the space reached full illumination, the ceiling emerged from the shadows. It was a dome with arches that met in the middle, covered in a series of beautiful paintings depicting the Mist Elf villages, the mountain, the lake, and the forests. The images were all rendered with a beauty that spoke of a mixture of magic and talent, which was an art some of the mystics pursued. *Was this here before the mystics, or are they somehow involved in the* venamisha?

She stood near the entrance, hands on her knives and her gaze on the pictures for long enough to realize she'd become entranced and lost track of time. Ruby shook her head, thinking about the tongue-lashing Keshalla would give her if she knew she'd let her defenses down that way, although the force shield was still active. She walked clockwise around the room, examining each statue in turn, interrogating them with both her mundane senses and her magical ones. The first was the Oriceran version of a deer, much like the Earth animal, rearing up on its hind legs as if attacking a threat in front of it. She ran her hand over the work, the carving so perfect and detailed that it almost felt alive. The eyes were sapphires, again so meticulously detailed that if not for their color they could be real.

That's not creepy at all. She suppressed a shudder at the feeling that something alive was trapped in the immobile rock and moved on. All the statues appeared carved from the mountain's native stone, and as positioned, none of them could retain their balance only by the force of gravity. There had to be magic at play in the chamber if only to keep the astonishing works of art from tipping over. The next was of a woman who looked very much like a Mist Elf except for the sharp pointed teeth she bared in a grin and the tentacles that stuck out from her scalp in place of hair. Her hands held fire as if she would hurl it at an unseen enemy. She was a creature from a children's tale, a siren that lurked under the waves to draw innocents to a watery grave. The siren's eyes were carved jade. This time the chill raised gooseflesh on her arms.

Ruby muttered, "Come one and all to the house of nightmares. This would make a hell of a sideshow attraction." The third statue was a tiger rearing up as the deer had. Shadows, ridges, and maybe different colors of rock indicated the stripes; she couldn't tell. The muzzle seemed twisted in something that almost looked like a superior smile. It was so lifelike that she backed away from it reflexively. The eyes of this one were crimson, carved from a scarlet gem, and instead of a round pupil like the Earth version possessed, this one had the slitted pupil of a domestic cat.

Ruby stepped quickly to the fourth statue, which she was pleased to discover didn't look as if it was going to attack or eat her. It was a mystic in long robes with an impressive beard, his eyes straining upward as if looking for wisdom. It held flames in its upraised palms like the siren and seemed to be trying to peer into them, or through them. The eyes on this one were flat stone, no jewels. She frowned, wondering what the difference was, then shrugged. *Not enough evidence to draw any conclusions.*

The voice in her head suggested, "Maybe when someone who's called dies, their spirit is trapped in one of the statues. Think about it. You could be here for eternity."

We *could be here for eternity. Also, shut the hell up.* The situation was challenging enough without her overly critical sense of self-awareness helping matters along. *I could be at home playing video games, but no, I had to be called to a dusty, dangerous, weird place under a mountain.* She walked to the final statue, which was the most unsettling of them all.

It was from another legend, a creature of the forest. The figure resembled a Mist Elf, but with bark for skin and leaves for hair. He appeared to be wearing armor, and the handles of six knives were visible at his hips, thighs, and boots. His face was arrogant, and he seemed to be looking down his nose at her no matter where she moved from side to side. His eyes were carved diamonds, and his lips framed a scowl. She got the feeling he would prove a formidable opponent, skilled in both magic and combat, and was very glad that he wasn't alive, despite how much the statue might try to convince her he was.

She reversed her direction and examined the statues again. None of them seemed any different on the second pass, so she returned to the only one that was unique, the one with the stone eyes. Ruby ran her hands over it to see if her eyes told a different story than what was physically there, as it was doubtful any illusion would stand up to two of the Mist Elves' senses. Nothing registered, but when she touched the figure's face, a chill breeze swept through the room. She stepped back, ready to fight or run, moving slowly toward the exit.

Ruby was halfway there when a door rose from the floor to seal it off. She ran to a wall and put her back to it, drawing and positioning her sword in a diagonal guard in one smooth motion. A kindly voice emanated from somewhere above. "Welcome, *junra*. You have reached your destination, and the object of your calling awaits."

She snapped, "Maybe you could be a little less creepy about it, huh?"

The voice didn't reply to her comment but continued in the same tone. "Before you can depart, you must endure the trial. Only those who prove themselves worthy may leave this place."

"Jerk."

"Those of us who have gone before wish you well, *junra*."

Her adrenaline surged through her veins, and she forced herself to remain calm. She'd seen enough James Bond movies to know that it could be anything next: flooding the room, lasers, maybe poison darts. Her mental voice added, "Or bees. Or spiders. That would suck."

You *suck*. *Shut the hell up.* The room changed again as she sensed another presence, or motion, or both. She scanned wildly, looking first at the thing that had given her the most visceral scare, but the siren with her nasty hair-tentacles was still in place, still immobile. A sound from her right caused her to turn in that direction, and she saw the forest warrior step forward. He turned to her, bowed, and drew the knives from his knee-high boots. They were longer than she'd imagined, almost short swords. Some keen sense told her he probably wouldn't put a force shield over the edges to protect her.

Fine. I'll do it myself. She'd never tried the idea, but it shouldn't be too hard. Ruby had anchored spells to objects before. It was part and parcel of creating magical items. In this case, she'd need to power it up, attach it to the blade, and let it run. Sure, it would be a continuous draw, but she could handle it if she didn't expend too much other magic. If he couldn't cut her, it would go a long way toward evening the odds since she was fighting a creature made of stone.

She envisioned and cast it in a matter of seconds. Her

jaw dropped in astonishment as nothing happened. For the first time in her life, other than when in the proximity of a powerful anti-magic emitter, Ruby couldn't access her power. Her foe grinned as if he'd been waiting for that realization to hit her, then lurched into motion much smoother than a stone being should have been able to pull off.

"Holy hell. I'm dead." Naturally, at the moment she could have used some intervention from her mental voice, a little confidence, maybe an ego boost, silence reigned.

CHAPTER FOURTEEN

While a small part of Ruby's mind might have decided the fight was over and she'd lost, most of it leapt into action thanks to a combination of stubbornness and long training. She shuffled quickly to her left, circling the brazier with her opponent walking after her like the gods-damned Terminator, that arrogant smile on his lips, and the stone knives that appeared sharp as steel in his hands. The fact that he didn't blink, only stared ahead with those diamond eyes, was as creepy as anything else about the situation.

Her mind catalogued his movements while she avoided him. He advanced in fits and jerks, which would help her recognize attacks, but he looked far faster than he should be. It seemed downright unfair that she couldn't use magic while he was obviously magical. She tried fire, shadow, and frost in quick succession with zero effect. Even her fall-back protection was now suspect since the amulet probably wouldn't work under whatever anti-magic field was in operation.

Okay, then, I'll have to beat down this rockhead on my own.

Fine. If I'm lucky, the sword will act like one although he's stone. If not, I'll chip away until he's dead. Or something. It wasn't a great plan, but it was the only one she had. She took one more shuffle-step away, then used her forward foot to push her into a run at her opponent, hoping her speed would lend her an advantage against the living statue.

He pivoted, and his lead arm came down in a block to protect his torso, but that wasn't her target. She slid at the last instant, wincing as the hard stone floor slammed into her leg, and slashed her sword across as she passed. It smashed into her enemy's ankle and chipped off a piece of rock but otherwise failed to accomplish anything useful. The statue lifted a foot to stomp on her, but she rolled away before it landed and got back to her feet. *Well, that sucked.* At least she knew that she could damage it, but it would take a while to evade its defenses enough to cut off its foot, which was likely her best option. *Even then, he'll probably stump around the place after me, or grow a new one, or something equally annoying.*

She backpedaled as he attacked, easily picking off the thrusts and sweeps of his knives. He surprised her by hurling one at short range, but she'd practiced defending against that particular move a zillion times with Keshalla and deflected it with a slight twist of her sword. He had another blade in his hand almost instantly, and they continued their progression around the room. She tested other parts of his body, slashing at the neck, the ribs, a wrist. None was any more effective than the attack on the ankle had been. When her mental voice finally joined the fight to observe, "We might be screwed," she couldn't disagree.

A swift set of strikes forced her to dive aside, and her shoulder complained as she rolled on it. She came up facing the deer-equivalent statue and was utterly surprised to see a weapon lying at the base of it, a forked antler that appeared to be metal. Her opponent drove her away from it with sweeping slashes, and she spotted more weapons on the next two statues. The siren had a chain and a trident, both of which were similar enough to weapons she'd trained with that she could use them. When she saw what lay at the foot of the tiger sculpture, she dashed for it, her desire for its offering overwhelming.

She snatched up the gauntlet at a run and slipped it on over her left hand, instinctively knowing that's where it would fit. Each of the fingers ended in a long claw, like the tiger she was borrowing it from might have. She slid her sword into its sheath and drew a knife, committing to keeping the rest of the fight up close where she could use the new weapon. *It has to be here for a reason, right? It has to be able to hurt that thing, or why bother?* She'd retrieved the knife mainly for blocking. Fortunately, Keshalla believed in unarmed combat and ambidexterity, so Ruby was well-positioned for the battle ahead.

Her foe's stone face didn't change, but he seemed to move faster as he darted in and sliced at her in a flurry of blows that she was hard-pressed to defend. She evaded some, deflected others with her knife, and finally had no option but to grab the one coming in at her eye with the gauntlet. Her opponent's weapon snapped in her hand, and a smile blossomed on her face. "Oh, that's not good for you at all, is it?" He had another weapon in his hand in seconds, but not before she landed a solid slash across his neck. The claws cut through like the statue was made of wood rather than rock, and while she would have preferred something softer, pudding maybe, she could cope. The blow left a trio of gashes that looked deep, and a small part of her brain deeply resented that statues didn't bleed.

Her foe expressed neither pain nor worry, only kept coming at her. He slashed with the knife, and she jumped back to avoid it but ripped his arm with her claws. He thrust low, and she blocked with her blade then stabbed forward with the talons. She realized her mistake as his other elbow slammed down on her forearm and caused the arm to go numb for a moment. *Feels like there's something fractured in there. Can't let him do that again.* She was more careful in the follow-up exchanges, only countering when it was safe to do so, and eventually it came down to one last blow. She blocked and leapt while slashing at his neck. When the statue's head fell off from her claws' final impact on the portion that remained, the figure vanished, only to reappear in its regular spot. She sank to the floor and downed her healing potion, gritting her teeth against the pain as her bones moved back into position before the wash of comfort spread over the injury.

She held up the claws, admiring them, and probably would have continued to do so if not for the throaty, feminine growl from behind her. "Take off the glove." She turned to see that the tiger statue had transformed into true life, a tiger that could somehow speak and was prowling toward her.

Ruby tried to summon a shield but still couldn't. "Uh, okay, sure. Nice giant tiger." She pulled off the gauntlet and stood after setting it down on the floor, then backed away. "There you go."

The tiger sat behind the gauntlet and stared at Ruby. The cat's fur was orange, gold, and black, and resembled the Earth species but somehow conveyed her magical nature. Maybe it was the slitted eyes, which stayed locked on her as the tiger swiped at the gauntlet and it vanished.

Ruby frowned and crossed her arms. "Hey, not fair. Why do you get to do magic?"

"I *am* magic."

"Well, so am I."

The creature snorted at her and shook its oversized head. "No, you *have* magic. I *am* magic. There's a difference."

Ruby nodded. *Okay, crazy cat. Whatever you say.* "Sounds good. So, what's the way out of here?"

The tiger lowered herself to lie on the floor with her paws underneath her. "The only way out is through."

"Through what?" She looked around the room, hoping to find that another tunnel had materialized. Nothing was any different, though, except for the fire in the brazier, which had started to burn a little less brightly.

"Through me." Laughter colored the words.

Fear stabbed through her. The tiger surely outweighed her by hundreds of pounds, and without her magic to protect her, Ruby wouldn't be able to take more than a couple of blows before succumbing. "Okay. How about rock, paper, scissors?" The look the tiger threw at her would have withered a less confident person. *Not me. I'm full of confidence.* "No, uh, Monopoly? Parcheesi? Go Fish?"

The tiger climbed to her feet again, then stretched and

yawned. And, improbably, kept stretching. Her body elongated and shrank until a Mist Elf woman stood before her, but with the same orange, gold, and black in her hair. She was covered with fur as well, except for her face, which looked normal. Her eyes were still those of a cat. Her voice sounded higher in this form as she said, "No, you must only answer a question. If you get it right, the door to exit this place will open. If you get it wrong, it won't. I'll go back to where I was before your entrance summoned me here, and you'll eventually starve to death if you don't go insane and end yourself first."

Ruby considered attacking the creature, but only for a moment. The tiger-woman would doubtless be less powerful in this form than in the other, which might give her the edge she needed to win. Then she thought about how easy it would probably be for the tiger to revert to all cat, or maybe only regain her claws. The wry smile on the other woman's face revealed that she knew exactly what was going through Ruby's mind. "Okay. What's the question?"

"Do you suffice?"

She blinked. "What?"

The other woman laughed at her, and Ruby took note of the sharp teeth that had hidden behind her lips. "Do. You. Suffice?"

She considered what the question would mean, coming from this magical creature. Could she defeat her in combat, maybe? She'd already won a fight, so perhaps the answer was yes. By most accounts, she'd been successful in most of the things she'd seriously tried to be good at in life. Was that the same as being sufficient? She thought back to the items her teacher had insisted she bring, the rations and water that she would have forgotten, not to mention the extra weapons and armor. *No, I most certainly do not suffice.* Still, was that the correct answer, although it was the true one? *Only one way to find out.*

"No. I do not suffice. I need others in my life to help me."

The tiger-woman grinned and nodded. "The beginnings of wisdom. Very good. You may call me Idryll." It sounded like eye-drill, and that's what the other woman's gaze was doing to hers.

"Okay. Hi. I'm Ruby."

"Interesting to meet you, Ruby." She gestured, and a door at the far end of the room opened to reveal a passageway. A passageway leading steadily upward, it appeared.

Ruby sighed. "Looks like I have a walk ahead of me."

Idryll nodded. "Indeed, we do."

Ruby blinked. "We?"

The woman laughed again as she shifted back into her tiger form, and again her cat mouth looked strange as she spoke. "Indeed, *we.* As you said, you do not suffice. From here on out, I will make up what you lack."

She couldn't put thoughts together, only followed the tiger as it led the way out of the room, its muscles rippling. *Fine. This is fine. Surely, this is fine.*

CHAPTER FIFTEEN

Enough time had passed inside the mountain that when Ruby stepped back through the portal from Oriceran to the kemana, it was the middle of the night. Rather than waking the family, she'd left a note to let Matthias, who was always the first to rise, know she was home. When she finished that, she discovered the tiger-woman was already asleep on the bed with the covers pulled up to her neck, making strange happy-sounding growly noises.

She changed into a nightshirt and climbed in beside her, wondering how in the world she'd explain this to everyone. Her head spun with the implications—how would they live together in the small attic room? What would her parents think? How much would she have to take care of her new apparent life-partner—until her brain succumbed to sleep, crushed under the burden of questions without answers.

She woke with the sun and stumbled toward the shower with a small growl of her own at the woman taking up far more than half of their shared sleeping space. When she emerged, toweling off her hair, Idryll was sitting cross-legged on the bed staring at her. Ruby stammered, "Uh, good morning."

She inclined her head in response. "The same to you, Ruby."

Again, she seemed faintly amused. Ruby wondered if something about her entertained the shapeshifter or if the other woman thought everyone on Earth and Oriceran existed solely for her amusement. "So, we never got around to discussing what you eat or any of that stuff." They had a veritable mountain of *stuff* to deal with.

Idryll shrugged, seemingly unconcerned. "I can eat anything in any of my forms."

"You, uh, have more than the two?" Ruby couldn't remember feeling quite so out of her element, *ever*, except when she'd met Keshalla for the first time.

Her laugh was throaty and inspired a smile despite Ruby's nervousness. "Oh yes, more than two. Are all humans as easily unbalanced as you are?"

Ruby scowled. "Well, if you mean would the average human find having a fatal headache that could only be fixed by fighting to the death to somehow wind up with a crazy cat lady as a life-partner somewhat disconcerting, yes. Also, I'm not a human."

Idryll lifted an eyebrow. "You look like one."

It was true. She was back in disguise now that they were on Earth. "That is a long, complicated, and as yet not completely revealed story. You know very well that I'm a Mist Elf, so knock it off." She sighed. "My mother will want all the details. Maybe *you* can tell her."

The other woman showed her teeth. "Oh, no. Also, you might find that you have…issues sharing any information about your *venamisha*."

Ruby frowned. "What kind of issues?"

Something like a purr came from Idryll. "The kind that will prevent you from speaking about it in any detail. There's a reason the stories are so vague."

A sigh escaped her. "Well, I guess I'll point at you, and everyone can figure it out for themselves. Now, come over here. We need to find you some clothes. I mean, your fur is nice and all, but you're going to distract every male who sees you if you don't put something on over it."

The other woman laughed throughout the process, which made Ruby grind her teeth. It felt less like a joyful laugh, although some mirth was in it than a condescending one. She'd never been particularly comfortable being the source of others' amusement, and that now included the oversized feline. Plus, it would take time to explain stuff, time she didn't have. She needed to get jobs lined up and put her business plans in motion, not to mention trying to figure out the next steps to make whoever killed the people at the casino pay for doing so. *I'm way too busy to deal with a person-sized talking cat with an attitude.*

When they were both properly clothed, Idryll stared at herself in the mirror while Ruby tamed her hair, pulling the still-damp locks back into a ponytail. A small chime echoed through the house, the staff's announcement that breakfast was ready. Except on special occasions, they never had a formal meal to start the day, which meant that the staff treated this as a special occasion, doubtless at her mother's request. "Lovely," she muttered, then continued, louder, "Okay, kitty, let's do this."

Idryll replied, "Perhaps don't call me kitty, and maybe I won't bite your arm off while you sleep."

"Yeah, yeah, whatever." She pulled open the door and headed out into the hallway. "This is fine. I'm sure this will be fine."

She steadily ignored the other woman on the way down to the dining room, then drew a deep breath and turned to warn her new partner not to cause trouble. She couldn't because Idryll wasn't there. She spun a full circle, wondering where she'd gone before the low rumble of a loud purr brought her eyes down to her feet. There, sitting primly beside her in a puddle of clothing that no longer fit, was a cat. She was a Bengal, probably twice as large as the usual breed, and had stripes like Idryll had in her tiger form rather than the more common spots. Even at that size, her amused superiority was obvious.

Well, that's useful, I guess. Mental note, put in an order at the pet store. She shook her head and whispered, "You are such a jerk," then turned and walked into the room. Only her father and sister were present, and Morrigan immediately shot to her feet and rushed over. Ruby grinned and held out her arms for a hug, but her sibling ignored her completely.

Her sister slid to her knees and enthused, "Oh my goodness, what a cute kitty. You're a sweetheart, aren't you? I know you are." The cat fell over on its side so she could pet it, and Ruby rolled her eyes and headed for the table.

Her father grinned at her. "You went on a legendary journey and what you have to show for it is a cat?"

She nodded as she sat. "It looks that way." She tried to tell him about it but discovered that the words wouldn't come. Confused, she made another attempt but still failed. "It appears there's a reason you don't hear about them more often. I try to explain, but no sound comes out."

Disappointment flickered across his face, but understanding quickly replaced it. "That explains a lot. Maybe you can answer questions. Let's try that. Is the cat part of your journey?" She nodded, happy to be able to confirm it. "Was it hard?" She nodded again. "Did you have to fight?"

She tried to nod a third time but was unable to move her head and laughed ruefully. "Seems like you've gotten all you're going to get from me, Columbo."

Rayar chuckled and nodded. "Well, okay then. This will really upset your mother, though."

Ruby laughed again. "Well, at least there's one bright spot. This time I get to keep the secrets."

Discomfort was there and gone in her father's expression, but he pretended it hadn't happened. "Will your roommates be okay with you bringing in a pet?"

She frowned and paused in the transfer of scrambled eggs from a bowl to her plate. "That's a good question. I have to hope so. They're pretty cool. I'm sure we can work it out."

Morrigan took her seat again. "Well, if not, I'm happy to keep her. What's her name?"

"Idryll."

Her sister scowled. "Where did you come up with that? It's rather vicious-sounding for such a pretty kitty." Her voice went sing-song at the end as she looked down to the side, presumably where said kitty was.

"She's volatile. Big claws."

"No way. She's adorable. She can stay here. We'll convert your room into a play area."

Her mother came in and immediately joined the chorus of approval over the new animal. Ruby's inability to divulge any exciting information about her experience was a major irritant for the older woman once she got past the suspicion that her daughter was being obstinate and refusing to share. *Like I would do such a thing. So, a little good, a little bad. Now I need to get the heck out of here.*

It took another half-hour before she could extract herself from the family and portal to the garage near the house she shared with her roommates. She escorted the cat up to her room, thankful not to encounter anyone along the way. When the door was closed, Idryll transformed into her tiger-woman form when Ruby turned her back. "This is where you live? I like the other place better."

"Shut it."

"I mean, why pink? It's not a shade that goes well with your skin. Makes you look rather sickly."

Ruby sighed. "Everyone's a critic. Listen, I need to meet with someone, and it's the sort of meeting where bringing a cat, a tiger, or another person along wouldn't make sense. Can I trust you to behave yourself here while I'm gone?"

The other woman threw herself back on the bed, which creaked underneath her alarmingly. *She must be heavier than she looks in this form. I don't want to explain that I managed to break my bed. Too good a setup for the others. I'll never hear the end of it.*

"Depends on how you define 'behave,' I suppose. I promise not to eat anyone unless they attack me first or I get really hungry." She looked thoughtful for a second and added, "Or bored."

"You know, I'd like to think you're only screwing with me, but something tells me you'd be downright dangerous to everyone around you if you lacked distraction." A small television sat on one of the dressers, and she flicked it on and handed over the remote. "Here, watch some TV. It'll be educational."

The tiger-woman pushed herself up on her elbows. The way her fur blended with her skin was beautiful. No clear separation between the two was visible although part of her was furred and the rest wasn't. "Do you expect to be gone long?"

Ruby shook her head. "I need to get to the Strip and call a car. Where I'm going is about twenty minutes away, figure an hour there, then the same back unless I find a good hidden spot to portal from. So, a couple of hours tops. Do you think you can manage not to ruin my relationship with my roommates for that long?"

Idryll leaned back with a long-suffering sigh. "I suppose. There better be something exciting waiting for me on the other side. Or I'll have to eat someone."

Ruby laughed. "Maybe I should introduce you to Jennifer then. Seems like a fitting end. Her gravestone can read, 'consumed by boredom.'" She walked to the door and pointed at her new partner. "Seriously. You behave."

The toothy grin she got in reply did not inspire confidence.

CHAPTER SIXTEEN

The trip had been more or less what she'd predicted. The car dropped her off at a town too small to be included on most maps. It sported a collection of homes, a grocery store, a gas station, a school, and not all that much else. She'd first visited Vagrant's Crossing when she was in high school as part of a career project and had returned every time she'd come home from university for a visit.

She looked up the long sidewalk that led to Margrave's house. "Phineas Margrave the Fourth," he'd declared at their first meeting, then insisted that she call him Margrave. High school Ruby couldn't be that informal, so they'd met in the middle with "Mr. Margrave," but the title had fallen off as she'd gotten older and they'd gotten closer.

Like Ely, the town was positioned at the base of a mountain, giving it a robust irrigation system. The lawns were green and expansive, a source of evident pride for the residents. Her business mentor's also bristled with odd statues and structures. He claimed it was his hobby: both the creation of artwork out of discarded junk, like the ten-foot-high skeleton made of what looked to be mainly car parts, and collecting items to tell stories, like the small forest of lawn gnomes engaged in a game of miniature croquet on the opposite side of the yard.

She noticed he'd added a new scene since her last visit nine months prior. Two homemade robots looked down over a chessboard filled with kid's action figures from old cartoons. One of the robots winked at her while she stared, and she laughed and bounded up the short stairs to the porch.

The man she'd come to visit opened the door before she reached it. Although he was in his fifties, he looked very well preserved for his age, upright and energetic. He had bushy brown hair, a bushy short brown beard, and a thin handlebar mustache curled back to point at his nose. He always wore jeans, t-shirts, sandals, and oversized flannel shirts, even in the hottest weather, and today was no exception. His enormous grin was a sign of his affection for her.

The one that stretched her face was for him, as well. She closed the remaining distance and gave him a hug, which he returned with strong arms. Finally, she stepped back, and he made a show of examining her. "Doesn't seem like graduating has changed you much. Did you get my gift?"

Ruby laughed. "Yes. The other folks I shared a house with at school weren't excited to discover such a small statue could contain so *many* confetti cannons, not to mention the sheer quantity of the stuff they spewed out."

He giggled—it was the most incongruous thing about him, that sound, and she adored it. "The secret is in the packing. You use magic to take out the air in between so you can get a nice tight arrangement."

She frowned. "How do you keep it from sneaking back in?"

He twirled one of the curls in his mustache. "Well, you have to work in a vacuum."

"You know how to create a vacuum?"

A slightly sheepish look crept onto his face. "Well, it required some experimentation. A little breakage, a burn or two, but no real, lasting danger. Anyway, it worked in the end." He waved her inside and led her straight into the basement, where he kept his workshop. His work area's illumination was battery-powered with lanterns and lamps on every surface, plus movable task lighting for specific needs. Down the center ran a long stone table, the size of two large picnic tables, but higher and polished to a perfect shine. It was soapstone, chemically inert by nature and magically inert due to a hell of a lot of work making it so. Margrave was both a wizard and an engineer. He was essentially what she wanted to be when she grew up, minus the wand and the eccentricities that had crept into his personality. *Or maybe they were there all along, and it doesn't have to do with all the "experimentation."*

Shelves and cabinets covered all the walls, their flat surfaces liberally adorned with components and parts, pieces, and who knew what else that the man used in his builds. Margrave created purely mundane objects on occasion, but his real interest was crafting items that blended magic and technology. As often as not, he made them as toys or for his entertainment, but she knew he also took challenging commissions that apparently paid well enough to give him lots of free time to pursue the things he loved. He'd never volunteered specific information about the business side of his craft, and she'd known not to ask for anything more than he was willing to offer freely.

Today, she had things to ask. Important things. "I need a little help with something."

He nodded and gestured at a stool positioned at one corner of the table, then took the one diagonally across from it at the end. "Of course. What can I do for you?" He grabbed a small metal file sitting on the stone surface and twirled it in his fingers—his energy always sought an outlet, and if he weren't deep in thought or work, he would inevitably fiddle with something.

"Two things. First, I have a weird question for you. Did you hear about the robbery attempt at the Mist?"

He gave a thin smile. "We may be backward out here at the crossing, but we're not *that* backward. We do get the news. Not to mention social media at 5G speeds."

She blinked. "You have 5G? How did you manage that?"

"Trade secret. It was a pretty puzzle. Took me a week to figure it out."

Ruby stared at him with a practiced look that almost always got people to keep talking. Unfortunately, he was immune to it, and like most things about him, change was unlikely. Finally, she shrugged. "Quit trying to distract me. What do you know about the casino?"

"I hear the explosives were partially magical. That's how they hid them."

"Holy hell. That makes sense. Still, I saw those guys, and there's no way they were magicals."

He chuckled. "I thought it might have been you when I

heard about the white-haired woman who beat them down. You asking about the robbery more or less confirmed it. What do you hope to accomplish now by trying to find out more? Closure?"

Only after she slammed her palms down on the table and shouted a curse did she realize how much anger and frustration she'd carried since the event. Angry tears leaked from the corners of her eyes as she composed herself again. "Sorry."

Margrave nodded. "It's okay. You can always be yourself here."

If only. Doubtless the man had sensed her disguise at some point but had chosen not to remark upon it. Given the work they'd done together, him teaching her how to make objects that incorporated magic and demonstrating how to combine the two, it would be virtually impossible for him to miss it. He'd never asked, and she'd never told. It was one of the reasons she trusted him as much as anyone on the planet. "I can't stop thinking about the fact that people died because of it. I want to understand why. I need to make sure those responsible pay for it."

His voice was emotionless, and his gaze had sharpened. "What might that payment entail?" It seemed like an important question, so she thought about it for almost a full minute before answering. What would be the proper counterbalance for such a loss? Could *anything* be?

Finally, she managed to reply, "Justice."

His expression didn't change, but his eyes softened a little. "That's an answer I can get behind. So, if the explosives mixed magic and technology, there aren't too many people who could have done the work for them, assuming as you said that they probably didn't do it themselves. There's only one other than me who I'd trust with the job."

"That seems like a good start. By the way you said it, I don't get the impression you're best buddies with whoever it is."

He barked a laugh and shook his head. "That would be an appropriate way of stating it, for sure. It's Grentham."

Ruby's eyes widened in surprise. "Oh. Yeah. I guess not." The dwarf was as close as Margrave had to a nemesis. They'd found themselves in competition for jobs over the years and had very different opinions about what was appropriate and what wasn't. Frequently, when the wizard refused a job, the dwarf was more than willing to take it on. "I didn't realize he was still around."

Margrave nodded. "He works for Aces Security, one of the big contractors."

Ruby was well-acquainted with Ely's security companies since they were an essential part of all the casinos' operations. They competed with one another for the best gigs and were vicious in attempting to run their competitors out of business whenever an opportunity presented itself. That thought led to another. "Do you think the robbery was to cause the Sunshis to lose faith in their security people? Is it a business move?" The notion that something so petty might have cost innocent lives made her jaw hurt from the force of her clenched teeth.

"*Big* business, if it's simply business, but no way to tell."

She tapped a fingernail against her teeth while thinking. "Actually, there might be a way to tell. Stop by their offices. Have a look around."

He shook his head. "They're not likely to let you in

there. Even if you play the casino owner's daughter card, you'll only get into a meeting room."

"Well then, I won't ask. What can you give me to help?" She'd come mainly to talk to him about whether he knew of freelance gigs she could take on, for him or his clients, but now she had a much more important task. A *purpose*, even.

"Are you sure of this? Seems like it's risky as hell. Those guys have guns."

She grinned and reached over to slap him on the arm. "Yeah, but I have you. Now, what gadgets do you have around here to turn me into James Bond for the evening?"

She'd convinced him because Margrave clapped, spun up off his stool, and headed for the cabinets behind him. "I have just the stuff. Grentham and his friends won't know what hit them."

CHAPTER SEVENTEEN

Ruby retraced her path back to the house she shared with her roommates and exchanged greetings with the others. Demetrius caught her on the second-floor landing, near the stairs to the attic. He looked around, as if to be sure no one was listening, and leaned in to whisper, "There have been sounds coming from your room."

She put on what she hoped was a suitably apologetic expression. "I must have left the television on. That was stupid."

He moved his head back to a normal conversational distance. "Yeah, it didn't sound like television. More like walking around."

Oh, hell. Idryll, you dumbass. "Okay. I guess I have to confess. I, uh, took in a stray."

He grinned. "Well, well, well. My roommate is wilder than I thought."

Ruby rolled her eyes. "Not that kind of stray. Although she is quite attractive."

Demetrius fanned himself with one hand. "*She.* My, you are a liberated woman, aren't you?"

She slapped him lightly on the arm. "Oh-em-gee. Come upstairs, before you start spilling gossip all over the place."

He put a palm on his chest. "Are you suggesting I could be part of…a thruple?"

Ruby frowned. "What the hell are you talking about, Demetrius?"

"Ah, there's the innocent Ruby we all adore." He followed her up the stairs toward the attic. "A thruple. Three people as a 'couple.' You know, polyamory stuff."

"Sure, okay, whatever. No, I'm not inviting you to be a couple, thruple, quadruple, any kind of uple." She stomped a little to ensure Idryll heard her approach, although she couldn't imagine a situation where the tiger-woman wouldn't be aware of it. *Exactly what I'll find when I open the door is open to question, depending on how annoying she wants to be. No point taking on problems that haven't happened yet. That's what Keshalla always says.* Of course, her mentor never had to deal with a sassy shapeshifter, as far as Ruby knew.

She opened the door, and her new life-partner was there in Bengal form, sitting primly and staring at them as they entered. Demetrius knelt to pet her, and Idryll accepted it with an attitude of "I deserve this." *That's the cat side of her coming out.* Ruby snorted inwardly. "So, there you go. The mystery."

Demetrius observed, "She's very well kept, for a stray." The look in Idryll's eyes as she tracked Ruby's walk to sit on the bed promised trouble later.

"Sometimes you get lucky." *Other times, you get Idryll.* "We more or less bonded immediately, so now we're stuck with each other."

He stood. "Well, that does explain the noises, although I have to say, it sounded more like walking than a cat. She must have been jumping around or something."

"Could be. I think she likes to chase dust motes, and there are always some of those in an attic." His phone rang, and he pulled it out of a pocket and looked down at it, then answered it and headed down the stairs with a wave. Idryll banged into the door to close it and was immediately in her most human-like form again.

"He's cute. Will you be dating him?"

Ruby fell back on the bed with a groan. "It's a little early for that, although I agree, all the boys are pretty easy on the eyes."

Idryll sat beside her, then flopped down so her head was near Ruby's. "I look forward to seeing these boys. Also, if I hear 'stray' too often, you're going to find your favorite things shredded beyond recognition." She delivered the threat as a simple statement of fact. "I saw Wolverine on the television. Imagine if he got hold of your stuff, but with sharper claws."

It wasn't worth trying to explain the idea of fictional characters. Ruby was exhausted, and she had things to do that would require her to be awake during the early hours of the day. "I need to nap. I have to break into a security company tonight."

Before she drifted off, she heard the soft comment, "*We* have to break into a security company tonight."

Given that Ruby didn't generally engage in the sort of activities that involved creeping around in the darkness trying to remain unseen, it took a lot of digging through her clothes to find the right ones. Her black paratrooper jump boots laced up to the bottom of her calf, and the matching tactical pants that she'd worn during a brief stint dating a hiker tucked nicely into them. She went with a simple black t-shirt with vertical ribbing that was otherwise unadorned and put on a hoodie in the same shade overtop it. She gathered her hair into a warrior's knot and clipped it in place.

While she did so, Idryll poked through her belongings and found an outfit. She'd chosen the same color scheme, which was good, but the way the tennis shoes, jeans, and men's dress shirt Ruby had stolen from a boyfriend hung on her was almost comical. However, with one of her spare hoodies, this one in charcoal rather than full black, and a little magic to hide her fur, Idryll looked entirely human. Until she moved at least since her feline grace came through despite the outward trappings.

Ruby had considered arguing with her partner about the wisdom of joining her attempt on the security company, but none of the justifications made sense. She'd played them out in her mind, and pretty much every complaint could be answered with, "Well then, why are you doing it?" Without a good answer to that question, there wasn't a point in getting into it.

Ruby said, "Okay, we'll portal from here to the casino.

Then we'll have to walk a couple of miles. I don't want to call a car, and I'm not familiar enough with the area to get there by magic."

Idryll grinned. "I enjoy long walks in the moonlight. Perhaps I could be part of your thruple after all."

She sighed. "No more television for you. I can't even deal." A quick check confirmed that she'd locked the door, so no one should wander in and find them mysteriously vanished. She slid a black backpack over her sweatshirt, pulled up the hood to mostly hide her face, and opened the path to Spirit. "Move it, kitty cat."

Idryll hissed and showed her fangs, but hopped through without any additional fuss. *This is fine. This is* definitely *fine.* With a sense of foreboding, Ruby followed.

It took most of two hours for them to reach their destination. The moon was up, but clouds diffused its light enough that it wouldn't be a concern. The modern office park was located to the southwest of the Strip and housed a wide variety of companies that served the casinos and their customers. Warehouses galore, distribution centers for food and beverages, accountants and lawyers, and dotted throughout, security company compounds.

Each of the businesses had defenses, from a simple chain across the vehicle entrance to the legal firms' building to high fences and barbed wire protecting the warehouses. The domain of Aces Security looked ordinary from a distance, but Ruby was sure that they would have an enhanced set of anti-intruder measures in place, if only so they could point them out to potential clients. Dralen, for instance, would be quite impressed by such things, as they doubtless fit his view of what a security company *ought* to be.

She and Idryll had circled the rear of the buildings, staying in the shadows the entire time. Ruby had altered her illusion. She was still a human, but with a borrowed face. It was modeled upon an NPC from a video game she'd played, that seeming to be the safest way to avoid someone getting accused falsely if her image was somehow recorded. She'd also darkened her skin to Jennifer's tan coloring since it was reasonably fresh in her mind. Whatever she was at the moment, it certainly wasn't a ghost. If anyone saw her hair, it wouldn't give her away either since it was now a plain mousy brown.

Of course, all of that was at risk if she used other magic, which was why she'd brought an assortment of gadgets along for the evening's activities. She dug into her bag and pulled out a healing flask and an energy flask that she'd retrieved from the house on Oriceran earlier, and slipped them into one of her thigh pockets. A compact toolkit went into the one on the other leg. Next up, a leather bandolier with typical throwing darts that Margrave had modified with small vials in various colors. Finally, a small drone and a control device. She drew out the controller's antenna, which he'd said worked through line of sight when it could so it would be less likely to be detected.

Idryll asked, "What's that?" She had the sense to keep her voice down, which again probably shouldn't have come as a surprise. Cats of all kinds were predators and knew how to sneak up on prey.

"It's a way for us to get a high-angle view on their defenses, both mundane and magical." The drone itself was about as large as her cupped hands, a rectangle with four propellers and a sensing block that included a camera and who knew what else. She set it on the ground, then used the remote to fly it high. It rippled and vanished as a magical veil spread over it. "Huh. He didn't say it would do that. Damn, he's good."

Aside from two joysticks for elevation and direction, the controller only had two buttons on it. She pressed the first, and some areas on the screen glowed. "Looks like they have motion sensors all around the fence and on the building itself. The fence itself is probably alarmed or electrified. They're playing it smart, too. The roof has the sensors as well." *There goes the plan to get to the roof and sneak in that way.* "On the plus side, I don't see any cameras, and this thing didn't indicate any. Probably they don't want anyone being able to tap into the lines or the signal or whatever." She hit the other button, but nothing lit up. "Well, if this is working like it's supposed to, there are no external magical security precautions. That likely means we'll find some inside." She worked the sticks to bring the drone back down. "Margrave was sure that Grentham wouldn't leave the place undefended."

"Are we going to portal to the door?"

Ruby winced. *Yeah, that's a logical question, and all I have for it is an embarrassing answer.* "Here's the thing. I can only portal to someplace I've been. Like, someplace I've physically stood. I'm not sure why, and no one has ever been able to explain why some of my magic works differently than for other people. It's one of the reasons I studied what I did in school, although I didn't find any good answers there either. Anyway, long story short, I can't portal from here to there."

The tiger-woman's expression suggested she was holding back laughter. "So if I asked you to portal to a spot five feet from there, you couldn't do it?"

"No. I couldn't. I can do lots of other things though, including kicking your smug ass with a wide array of weapons and talents. Leave it, and let's get a move on."

Idryll shook her head. "What other things can't you do? Light candles? Make ice when it's hot outside?" She'd stuffed her hands into the pockets of her sweatshirt, as though conserving energy for what was to come, remaining almost still in the cool air. *Warming herself with the heavy application of mockery, apparently.* She asked, "So, we go in fast and hard, and kill any who oppose us?"

"No, we're still not opting for your plan." The shapeshifter had tried to sell her on that approach several times already. "There's no guarantee they're guilty, and if they're not, we'd be as much in the wrong as whoever killed those folks at the Mist."

"Are all of your people as impractical as you are?"

Ruby packed the drone into the bottom of the backpack so she'd have quicker access to a couple of other specialty items inside it and put it on her back again. "What you call impractical, the rest of the world calls 'logical,' or 'reasonable,' or, and I like this one best, 'not murderously insane.' Perhaps you could join us on the rational side of things for a while. See how it goes."

Idryll snorted. "Risking yourself for the benefit of others isn't rational."

"Shut it, and let's go." She headed in a crouched run for the nearest corner of the fence, one of Margrave's darts held in each hand.

CHAPTER EIGHTEEN

She felt the drain on her illusion as she neared the corner, what could only be an anti-magic emitter, and a strong one at that, and dropped to a knee. "Damn it. They *are* thoroughly prepared. Well, maybe it means there won't be any inside." She'd considered using a force blast to fly over the fence and into the compound but was thankful she hadn't. Having her ability to cushion her fall taken away would have been a pretty solid disaster.

She pulled the hood closer around her face as a shiver of anxiety flowed through her. The shadows were still significant, and the area didn't have spotlights, thankfully. *No, subtlety seems to be the rule so far.* The emitters took care of her original plan, which had been to use the darts and the spells they contained to knock out the motion sensors. She'd planned to use them on the cameras she'd expected to see, as well. *I hope they're not simply really well hidden.* Now, she needed a different idea. She whispered, "If we move slowly enough, we should be able to defeat the motion detectors. It won't be fun, but it'll be doable. I didn't bring bolt cutters though. I figured I'd use magic to deal with any barrier."

Idryll grinned and held up her hand. Claws extended from beneath four fingers, a slight shine the only thing that showed the black weapons in the darkness. "I can take care of that."

Ruby nodded. "Okay, we'll do it then. If we meet with trouble, we split up, hide, and meet at the house. It'll be bad if they catch me, but I can always fall back on my family. Them catching you would be much worse, especially if they realize what you are. Plus, a cat wandering around in the building once we get inside would probably be pretty damn suspicious."

"As if they could catch me."

"They have magic and weapons at their disposal and could always get lucky. It's not impossible."

The shapeshifter snorted in derision and crawled toward the fence, her body barely off the ground. Ruby followed, with notably less agility. Eventually, they reached the barrier, and Ruby hissed for the tiger-woman to stop. Placing her hand near the metal revealed no trace of the tingle that would come with proximity to electricity. Ruby had to admit to being surprised it wasn't electrified, but maybe out here with wildlife, workers coming and going at the other businesses, and who knew what else, that wasn't a practical choice. She pulled out a handful of cables with alligator clips and carefully connected the metal on either end of the spot where they'd make their entrance, ensuring that any circuit that existed from one side to the other still would when they cut the fence. She lifted the lines with a nod, and Idryll sliced through the chain-link with a single stroke of her claw.

It required a full hour of careful movement for them to cross the wide expanse of grass that separated the outer perimeter from the building. Ruby recognized a shooting range as they crawled through it, and also an obstacle course like the ones she'd seen in army movies. *Guess they use their backyard for training. Makes sense, really. No one to see what's going on, thanks to the fences, and as long as they warned their neighbors to expect the gunfire, no cause for alarm.*

She tapped Idryll's foot and pointed toward a small door set in the back of the building beside three huge windowless garage doors composed of the same metal skin as the rest of the place. Google Maps had shown the part of the facility visible over the fence as dark blue, and it seemed to be uniform over the whole structure.

They made it to the entrance without an issue. The anti-magic field generated by the emitters fell off about six feet away from the building. "There's going to be an alarm system attached to this door. I have a gadget that should confuse the signals enough that it looks like a malfunction that corrects itself rather than a break-in, but no guarantee that someone won't come to investigate. Remember, no killing."

"You're no fun at all."

Ruby softly snorted. "So I've been told." She dug in the pack for the small silver disc. It was thinner than a credit card and carried both force and electrical magic. There would be a three-second pause when she activated the device, long enough for her to get it wedged into the doorway, then discharge. The electricity would temporarily confuse most security systems, and if positioned properly, the force would push the door and frame apart enough that she could get it open. The physical deadbolt, which wasn't part of the alarm network, she'd deal with essentially telekinetically. In reality, it was very fine-controlled force magic, but if it looked like telekinesis and acted like telekinesis, she would go ahead and think of it as telekinesis. "Ready?"

Idryll grinned. "Since before you were born."

She scowled. "How long were you in that statue, anyway? I mean, I can see why someone would be so annoyed with you as to trap you in stone for a century or two. Hell, I'm there already, and I've only known you for what, two days?" Without waiting for a reply, she shoved the disc in, slid the deadbolt aside, and yanked the door open. Her partner slipped inside, and she followed, pulling the door closed behind her. She paused, ready to make a break for the back fence if they'd been detected, but no alarms came.

They were in a huge garage at least two stories high, with cars and trucks of several sizes parked in front of the exits. It reminded her of fire stations she'd seen in news broadcasts, minus the emergency pole from the upper floor. Three of the vehicles resembled armored cars like the ones a bank might use. All of them had reinforced bumpers and fenders for ramming and larger than expected wheels. "That's pretty damn martial, right there. Seems a little offense-focused rather than defensive to me."

Her partner intoned, "If your enemy is dead, they cannot hurt you."

"Not much room for negotiation in your world, is

there, kitty?" She could tell that calling the shapeshifter "kitty" got under her skin and was fully committed to doing so with reasonable regularity.

"A tiger doesn't negotiate with meat. Only eats it."

Then again, maybe pissing off the giant jungle cat isn't the wisest choice. "Okay, let's move on. Same rule. If we wind up in trouble, I want you to make a break for it since the worst I'll get is a slap on the wrist."

Her partner's tone failed to match her words. "As you wish."

Ruby sighed, then made sure the bandolier full of darts was properly situated. She positioned two of the electrical projectiles in her left hand, ready to disarm any modern surveillance devices they came across, and opened her senses in the hope that she might notice magical defenses before they activated. "Remember, we have a magical on the other team. There could be traps."

"Are you going to talk until sunrise, or are we going to move?"

She frowned. "You know, it's not like I make a regular practice of breaking into buildings. This is all kind of new to me. Consider not being a jerk." Still, truth lay within the cat's words since she had to admit she was procrastinating. *A little. Maybe.* "All right, let's do this."

Two doors led from the space, one on the near side and one across the vehicles' parking spots. They chose the nearest and moved through in a rush. Ruby flicked a dart at the camera in the corner the instant she spotted it, and the equipment gave a telling *sizzle* as the electrical spell in the projectile went off on impact. "Well, they'll know we're here soon enough if we keep having to kill cameras. There was no way to avoid that one." Fortunately, her disguise was back in place, and her partner had cinched her hood carefully around her face, hiding her fur. Idryll's claws had vanished as well, leaving her hands looking entirely human. *Yep, that's us, a pair of normal humans where we don't belong.*

The hallway led deeper into the building. They walked past conference rooms with glass walls, a small kitchen, bathrooms, and what looked like a combination locker room and armory abutting the other door into the garage. No other cameras were visible, which was a little alarming in and of itself. *Maybe they don't want a record of what goes on in here existing, and only cover the entrances and exits. That would make some sense, even if they're on the up-and-up.* A double-wide staircase led up from the back of an impressive lobby area, and they moved quickly up the steps.

Idryll hissed as they neared the top and abruptly stopped moving. Ruby halted immediately and dropped into a crouch. "What?"

The shapeshifter's face wrinkled as if she smelled something unpleasant. "Hostile magic. From ahead."

"You can smell magic?"

"Smell, taste, feel, hear, sense, all of those or none, I can tell you it's up there."

Well, that wasn't even a little understandable. Thanks for the illumination. "Okay, can you tell what kind?"

Idryll shook her head. "No. Only that it waits to be triggered."

Magical defenses were a large part of a techno-magical engineer's work, so she'd trained and become well-acquainted with various possibilities. She pulled out the drone, fired it up without letting it fly, and used it as a camera to examine the room. Sure enough, a tight grid showed up on the floor that was likely both detection and device. "Interlocking lines. Probably electrical, since they wouldn't want to burn the building down or anything." She showed the display to her partner.

"Could trigger weapons."

Wonderful. "You're right, it could. So, best we stay off it." She used the drone to examine it some more but discovered no other defenses in the room. "Here's my thought. I can create a force shield above it. We walk on the force shield and get through one of those two security doors." She put the drone and its controller away and pulled out a palm-sized square object. "This should pick the electronic lock in no time."

The other woman lifted an eyebrow. "So you say you've not broken into other places, but you have the tools to do so?"

She shrugged. "You have to learn a lot of things to become what I want to be. We used these as a basis for figuring out how to defeat magic locks. Not that we're quite there yet. This is more or less one-size-fits-all, but magic locks require far more specific countermeasures." She handed it over. "You hold it over the keypad. It should do the job without any other involvement."

She made sure to cinch her hood tightly and summoned a force shield above the grid. She'd never used one quite this way, but it wasn't a far stretch from things she was familiar with. Walking across it was difficult since she had to keep the part of her mind that sensed the steps on the shield segmented from the rest so she didn't get confused and drop it by accident.

They made it to the door, the lockpick did its work, and they were through. Right into a room filled with four security guards who were already in motion, abandoning the food containers on the round table they sat at in favor of grabbing weapons.

CHAPTER NINETEEN

Idryll bolted to the right as Ruby called, "Split up." She had no intention of abandoning the Mist-Elf-pretending-to-be-human that she'd joined with, despite the repeated suggestion that she do so. The mere concept was ludicrous, but the other hadn't quite realized the repercussions of undertaking the *venamisha*. *She has no idea what she's in for.*

At times, the ritual battle resulted in a mismatch where the choice of weapon paired the pilgrim with someone who wasn't right for them. Those people would have false memories of the experience and would return more or less to everyday lives, convinced that their calling hadn't turned out to be a true one. *Better that than a lifelong bond that would make both parties miserable.* When the person chose wisely, as Ruby had, the benefits to both partners were incalculable.

Like now, when she's stumbled into a situation that might have been dangerous for her if I weren't here. Her natural inclination was to transform into her tiger form and tackle several of them at once, but the clothes would be a problem, and there was no reason to reveal that power to deal with this trash. One enemy was directly in front of her on the same side of the table and bringing a pistol up from his hip. Her instincts told her he had no chance of getting it into action before she reached him though, so she ignored it. On the opposite side of the furniture, the second fumbled with a larger device she didn't recognize. Her knowledge of human weapons was limited to what she'd seen on the television.

However, it was probably safe to assume that increased size often meant increased danger, as with most things. *I'll deal with that one first.* She smoothly leapt into the air and tucked her knees up against her chest. The jump took her over the first opponent, and she had a split second to be amused at his expression before she was past him. She kicked back with both feet, wishing she had claws instead of sneakers—they made far too much noise to sneak in compared to her paws, so that was a stupid name—to do real damage. The feel of the contact assured her that he'd be flat on his face for at least as long as it would take her to handle the other, who she now flew toward even faster after using the first as a platform.

The man with the longer weapon got it around to point in her direction, but it was too low for him to shoot her with it, if that's what it did, and it certainly wasn't in a position to be used as a club. Her right hand grabbed the thing to ensure that the angle didn't change, and she brought her other one across so that her elbow smashed into him. She'd aimed for his throat, only remembering after he'd managed to block that with his chin—now broken—that Ruby had requested she not kill anything.

Idryll showed her fangs in a smile and laughed inwardly. *Ruby probably thought it was more than a request. She* does *have a great deal to learn.*

Idryll rode her foe down to the floor, making sure that her full weight, transmitted through both knees, broke more of his bones. *He won't get back into the fight.* The first had risen faster than expected and pointed a gun at Ruby, who was at work on her second opponent. Idryll roared, the tiger's yell magically produced since this form's vocal cords couldn't create it. The man flinched, and his shot went into the ceiling. She was on him a second later, reluctantly keeping her claws sheathed as she swatted him in the back of the head, smashed a fist into his ribs, and slammed a foot down on his knee. He fell to the floor, and she gave him two kicks: one to knock his weapon spinning away, and another to roll his eyes back in his head.

Before she could turn to assist her partner, a door opened to reveal a man with a baton in one hand and a gun in the other. He charged at her while sticking the weapon out in front of him. She swatted it aside as she moved away from his gun hand and yelped in pain as lightning came out of the tip and surrounded her hand, burning it and making her muscles twitch. Ruby yelled, "Watch out, stun baton," and Idryll's teeth bared in a fierce grin. *A little late as a warning. I'll know one when I see it again.* The man tried to fire over his extended arm, but she ducked and spoiled his aim, then put a palm on the carpet and spun in a circle, sweeping his legs out from beneath him. She ripped his weapons away and threw them aside, grabbed him by the shirt, lifted him, and banged the back of his head off the floor, once, twice, and a third time, until he was unconscious.

She stood and turned to her partner, who had dealt with her pair. Ruby said, "We're sure to have set off alarms now. Let's see what we can find out before more bad guys show up." She led the way deeper into offices, using her little metal things to get the doors open and rifling through desk drawers while Idryll watched for additional enemies.

A sound came from the room they'd entered the level on. She crept back to look, then quietly returned to Ruby. "A lot of men, more than we fought before, are gathered in the entryway. I don't think we can beat them without risking injury."

Ruby snarled a curse and started shoving papers into her backpack. "Go to the other offices and bring me whatever papers you can find. I'll work on slowing them down." She dug into another part of her bag and came out with a handful of small globes, but Idryll lost sight of them as she raced down the hall. The first door proved resistant to her kick, so she summoned her claws and raked one through the gap between door and frame repeatedly until it came free. Two wire baskets, one on top of the other, sat on the desk. She grabbed them and returned to Ruby at a run, then dumped them into the backpack. Now four orbs sat in front of the door, and the other woman followed her back.

As they got the next doors open, using their different techniques, shrieking sound and flashing light came from the doorway. Ruby chuckled. "Hope they were wearing night-vision goggles. That would hurt. A lot."

"You are too gentle." Idryll dumped more papers into the bag. It was almost full.

Ruby nodded. "Only when I can be. These people are probably doing their jobs. Sure, they might be doing it for a bunch of scumbags, but that's not necessarily their fault. It's possible they don't know."

Idryll shrugged. "If you choose to follow a poor leader, still, that is a choice."

The other woman shifted the pack onto her back. "Is dealing with *you* a choice? If I say go away, will you?"

She laughed. "No. Nor would a smart person wish me to. Although perhaps your intelligence level has still to be determined."

Ruby put her mouth to Idryll's ear. "I had planned for us to portal out of here, but I'm not sure that's a good idea. I wouldn't want them to get even a little look at where we're going, and the lack of cameras makes me think they're probably there, but well-hidden."

"Perhaps there is hope for your intellect after all. I agree that they would be fools not to have surveillance everywhere."

The other woman ignored the jibe. "So, we'll go through them fast and hard. I'll blast them with force to clear the path, then we run back the way we came. No worry about setting off alarms outside. If we can get a decent distance away, out of their line of sight, I'll open a portal to a neutral location." She knew several points on the Strip that wouldn't be easily identifiable through an open portal, mainly service roads and alleys.

Idryll nodded. "I'll follow your lead."

Ruby ran forward and blasted the smoke that had filled

the hallway with force magic while covering her face with her free hand. It took two more blasts to clear the way as they bolted through, angled to deflect their opposition to the sides rather than directly back. She'd worried that the enemy Ruby had identified—Grentham—might be there, but probably these were people who had already been at the facility since they'd responded so quickly. Moving out before magical opponents could arrive was indeed wise.

Alarms blared as they went through the back door and into the motion sensor field. Ruby angled toward the hole in the fence, and for a moment Idryll wondered why, then remembered the anti-magic devices the other woman had mentioned. They weren't powerful enough to rob her of her abilities, and she felt them only as a small tickle at the edge of her senses. As she neared the fence, which was at least four times her height, she gathered herself and leapt, easily clearing it to land on the opposite side.

She helped pull Ruby through, and together they ran back the way they had come. Shouts and gunfire came from behind, but after the first *crack*, her partner placed a force shield around each of them, and they kept running. She shouted, "Do you think we got anything worthwhile?"

Ruby yelled back, "Not sure, but they seem like they wanted to hide something. That many people in the building for overnight security? If it's not a coincidence, it's probably worth following up. Hopefully, there's a clue in the papers we stole."

Idryll laughed. "Congratulations, by the way."

They rounded a corner, and Ruby stopped running and summoned a portal. They both hopped through it, and she closed it before any of the men chasing them showed up on the other side. After panting for a few seconds, she asked, "Congratulations? For what?"

She laughed again. "You said you'd never broken into someone's building before. Well, now you have. Doubtless it's the first of many new experiences now that you've chosen to oppose those who would hurt innocents."

She frowned. "I'm only trying to find out what happened at the Mist. Let's not make more of it than it is. Come on. We have a bit of a walk to get to Spirit."

Outwardly, Idryll nodded and followed without replying. Inwardly, though, she grinned. *Yes, partner, you have a lot left to learn. I'll be right here to help, every confused step of the way.*

CHAPTER TWENTY

Jared Trenton, CEO of Aces Security, angrily marched through the lobby and headed directly for the surveillance room, a small rectangle accessed through an unmarked door. He'd discussed the situation with Grentham the dwarf on the way in, and neither had a clear idea about what had happened the night before. It made the most sense to think that someone had connected them to the action at the Mist, but as far as he knew, the people he'd hired didn't have any clue who they'd worked for.

Grentham had no clue how anyone had created the link either, which was unusual. Normally, if Jared was clueless about something the magical had it under control, and vice versa. It was one of the things that made their partnership so effective. He had sales meetings lined up for the rest of the day, so instead of being able to get down into the details and investigate like he wanted to, he was in his lucky black pinstripe suit with a bright red power tie. His short brown hair had been trimmed the day before, his face was freshly shaven, and he stayed in shape, both as a personal preference and because the clientele expected it. The Mist's owners were bound to look for additional security now, and he'd scheduled his appointment with them a month in advance.

Almost as if I knew something would happen. He chuckled to himself. Inside the surveillance room, he found his partner looming over one of their technicians, a geeky man in his mid-twenties. Jared snapped, "What do we know?"

The dwarf replied, "Camera caught the perps, but it's not particularly useful." He was short, stocky, and dark. Dark hair, dark mustache, dark beard, dark eyes, dark clothes. He wore exclusively black, as near as Jared could tell. At the very least, he'd never seen the magical in anything else. His slicked-back hair and his carefully trimmed facial hair gave him an "evil magician from the movies" look. The black trousers, shoes, and dress shirt accentuated the effect.

Jared growled, "Show me." The technician mumbled and pointed at a screen where two thin figures in hooded sweatshirts stood frozen in time. It was impossible to tell anything about them from that angle. "Is that the best we've got?"

The dwarf replied, "Yeah. The cameras that would have gotten a good look at their faces had a malfunction." He handed over a small dart, and Jared held it up to the light.

"What's special about it, other than this clear piece?"

"That's the important part. It contained magic. Lightning. Shorted out the camera. The thrower was smart enough to keep their head down."

He grunted. "How did they get past the motion sensors?"

"I assume they were very slow and very patient. I don't imagine they overcame the anti-magic emitters or anything."

Jared frowned. "So you're saying they were magicals?"

Grentham nodded. "At least one of them, anyway. The camera caught them creating a force shield over my detection grid. Clever trick. How they knew the grid was there is a question I'd very much like to ask them."

He looked at his watch and frowned deeper. "Let's talk upstairs."

The invaders had fortunately not had time to make it to his corner office in the back. They might not have been able to get in even if they had, due to the complicated lock his paranoia had demanded. The room was better decorated than those of his subordinates but still downright spartan compared to the upper-level management in the casinos. File cabinets covered one wall, each with biometric security, and a couple of pieces of artwork depicting military scenes graced the others. His furniture was all wood and steel with four chairs around a meeting table, plus an L-shaped desk with a chair on either side.

Jared leaned forward on that desk and growled at the man across from him, "Do we have a leak?"

Grentham shrugged. If the anger radiating off his boss bothered him, he didn't show it. "I can't see how. Only you, Phillips, and I knew on our side, and there's no way he talked. He understands perfectly that reporting anyone contacting him will get him a bigger payday than going against us. Besides, we've seen no unusual activity from his surveillance."

The CEO grunted, leaned back in his chair, and ran his hands through his close-cut brown hair. The decision to keep eyes on his top-level subordinates wouldn't make any of them happy if they knew about it, so the dwarf took care of it personally. "One of the people we hired, then?"

"They couldn't have known about the connection back to us. If anything, the secrecy would have led them to believe they were working for *him*, and no way would they have said so." Even when they were alone, they didn't use that name because if someone got a hint of his involvement and he felt the slightest amount of risk, he'd sweep the field clean by killing them all and burying them in the desert.

"Okay. That makes sense. So, we chalk it up to random chance, with the possibility that one of our competitors put a word in someone's ear to make life difficult for us?"

Grentham tugged on his beard, a sign that he was thinking. After a few seconds, he nodded. "That seems like the only logical way to go. Of course, we'll beef up the defenses and add in some new wrinkles that will make that pair unhappy if they're stupid enough to come back, and I'll have the protection team do a full evaluation of our processes. They don't have much else on their plate right now, unfortunately."

Yeah, and that's the heart of the problem. When Jared had created Aces Security, it had seemed like a risk-free venture from the financial side. All those casinos plus the companies that supported them, working with lots of cash and materials, would need security to protect them. He had the contacts from his time in the military, good people who were willing to do what was required to take care of his clients. Early contracts were plentiful, but ultimately competitors came in, and some of the businesses switched providers. Eventually, he was running in the red rather than the black. *That's when I got the offer I couldn't refuse. Not that I would have anyway if there'd been an option.*

He nodded at the dwarf. "Well, we'll have to see what we can do about that. The next phase is ready to go?"

Grentham confirmed, "Yep. Scheduled for tonight."

"Excellent." Jared stood and adjusted his cuffs, feigning confidence he didn't feel. "I have a meeting with the wizards and witches about watching one of their warehouses."

"Pathetic. Scraps."

He shrugged. "We need cash flow, and we have the people." He didn't have enough work to keep his current staff busy, much less the additional personnel he'd been ordered to get on the payroll as quickly as he could manage. Grentham didn't know about that part of the overall picture and wouldn't if Jared had anything to say about it. *He knows enough about our ties to the big man. Any more, and someone might think I'm an accessory rather than an essential component. I'll see them all dead before I let that happen.* His watch buzzed with a message, and he stared down at it, first in irritation then in trepidation. In a rasp created by his suddenly dry throat, he said, "Looks like I'm going to be a little late for the meeting. Will you have someone push it back a half-hour?"

He steered the SUV into a parking spot right next to another that looked just like it. A half-hour before, he'd put his phone and watch into a box that would block all signals in or out so the electronics couldn't trace him, and flipped the switch that deactivated the vehicle's GPS sensor. As far as any records that might exist of his location, he was last seen in a fast-food parking lot near his business.

In reality, he'd driven south to a vast oil facility that had a private covered parking lot. His car had been expected because the guard at the gate lifted it before he had to roll down his tinted window to ask. He climbed out of his vehicle and into the passenger seat of the other one. The driver, a stocky human with a blond flattop, dark sunglasses, and an attitude that filled the small space nodded. "Trenton."

"Smith." All of his contacts with the organization that now more or less owned him after the initial meeting with the boss of all bosses were named something simple. He'd encountered two Joneses, one Anderson, and one Matthews so far, plus the Smith. In idle moments on the drive to and from meeting places, he wondered how they all kept it straight or if they required their people to adopt new names full time. "What's so urgent?"

The man's hand dipped into his suit coat, and Trenton tensed. They all dressed alike, too, with dark suits, white shirts, boots instead of dress shoes, and not a tie in sight. They also carried pistols in shoulder rigs. He only withdrew a sealed envelope with no name on it. "Orders."

He'd never for the life of him understand why the organization preferred in-person meetings to the more modern tools of the trade, like temporary emails, encrypted smartphone apps, or even burner phones. *Next up, we'll be doing freaking dead drops with chalk marks on the sidewalk.* He took the envelope without a word and put a twist of humor in his farewell. "Smith."

"Trenton." The other man nodded.

Jared climbed back into his vehicle and waited as the other one drove off. Then he opened the envelope and saw the two paragraphs of printed commands inside. *Holy hell. That's an escalation. On a compressed timeframe.* He gunned the engine and headed for the exit, afraid as always of failing the big man. In the recesses of his mind, a small, worried voice wondered what the next operation after this one would be and whether he'd survive it. *Time to make sure I've fully funded my escape stash and my go-bag is ready for a long trip on short notice.*

CHAPTER TWENTY-ONE

Ruby had slept fitfully for a few hours after their adventure, but she couldn't bring herself to stay in bed with all the possibilities running through her brain. Coffee and a shower helped, and she returned to her room to find Idryll sitting on the bed in her tiger-woman form, surrounded by paper. Her partner had worn one of Ruby's nightshirts to sleep in and looked as rumpled and tired as she felt. Now that Ruby was back in her standard jeans, boots, and t-shirt, at least her lack of focus should remain mostly hidden by the guise of normality.

"Found anything?" Then, belatedly, "Uh, would you like some coffee?" Ruby stepped near her and extended the mug.

Idryll leaned over and sniffed it. Then her lips pulled back in a frown. "No. Hideous. You find that appealing?"

"Well, it's not exactly Starbucks quality or anything, but yeah, I like it." So far, Ruby had managed to find the other woman things to snack on, and she seemed to prefer the grazing approach to eat instead of a big meal. "We'll get you something when we go out. Maybe stop at a breakfast place. Have you had pancakes?"

With her eyes on the papers, Idryll gave a slow head-shake. "I have found a reference on several of these things to something happening tonight and to a dark dragon."

"Ebon Dragon?"

"Yes, that's the phrase. Did I not interpret it properly?"

Ruby made a seesaw motion with the hand that wasn't holding the mug. "They mean the same thing, more or less, but Ebon Dragon is the name of a casino. A title."

"Ah." The tiger-woman nodded. "That makes more sense, then."

She frowned. "How do you know how to read the human language?"

Idryll lifted her gaze to meet Ruby's. "You understand it, so I understand it."

That's not creepy or anything. "Do you mean you know everything I know?"

The other woman made the same motion with her hand as Ruby had. "Not really. Say more that some things you do unconsciously I can also do. Conscious stuff is messy, and I can't get to it easily."

That goes in the "worry about later" file. "What do you mean by tonight?"

"There are references to sunset and to something called 2200." She said the numbers one by one.

"Twenty-two-hundred. That's military-speak for ten at night."

She held out a piece of paper. "Strange custom."

Ruby took it and saw that it was a printout of an email with only the time and a series of numbers. "Why do you think this has something to do with the Ebon Dragon?"

Idryll pawed through the papers on the bed until she found the one she wanted and presented it with a flourish. "The names are the same on this one, which includes those words."

She read the email, which seemed on its face to be nothing more than arranging a get-together to gamble at the casino. *In context with the other one, it could mean something. Or it could mean that they're spending the night gaming. It's the best we've got, I guess.* "Okay, so probably we should wander down and take a look at this place later. Is it possible for you to, uh, get rid of the rest of your visible fur? I mean, the hoodie look is a good one, but maybe not in the middle of the afternoon."

Her partner sighed. "If necessary, yes. It is uncomfortable to do so for long periods."

"I guess the alternative is that you could stay here."

"Not a chance. I'm about ready to start chewing on people from sheer boredom."

Ruby grinned. "We could stop by a store, get you a big ball of yarn to play with."

The sound of the door opening made Ruby's heart shoot into her throat, and she spun, ready to jump and block whoever it was from seeing the other woman. Daphne walked in, oblivious to the panic she'd caused, and her mouth dropped open for an instant before she shrieked, "Oh my God, it's so cute!" Ruby followed her gaze to see that the Bengal cat was back, rolling around on the bed to get free of the nightshirt that trapped it.

Her roommate rushed over and helped extract the

animal, then looked up at Ruby expectantly. She sighed. "She's a stray. Followed me home a couple of days ago." More or less true. "Now I can't get rid of her, even if I wanted to." Again, true as far as it went. "So, I guess we have a cat. She's not particularly friendly, though. Watch the claws."

Idryll, naturally, had shifted onto her back and was accepting belly rubs and nonsense noises from the witch. Ruby rolled her eyes but couldn't restrain a smile. *All things considered that went pretty well. Nicely done, kitty.* She asked, "Is there something I can do for you?"

Daphne nodded, not taking her eyes off the purring creature in front of her. "I wondered if you could deliver a package for me. I promised Abbot Thomas that I'd get it to him, but I got called into work. There's no way I can afford a delivery service right now, and I thought since you haven't lined up your freelance gigs yet, you might have an hour or two to take care of it."

Just like that, she was neatly trapped. Everything the other woman said was true although it didn't account for the time she was putting in as an amateur detective. "Of course, I'll do it. No problem."

With a sigh, the witch hopped off the bed and baby-talked at Idryll. "I wish I didn't have to leave you, pretty kitty." She turned to Ruby. "Instructions and directions are on the box. He knows it's coming, so you shouldn't have a problem. Thanks, roomie."

When the door closed behind their guest, Ruby said, "Now that she knows, everyone else will, too."

The Bengal laughed in Idryll's voice and spoke, the mouth movements even more disconcerting than when she did it in tiger form. "Good. Perhaps I can begin to get a proper level of appreciation, then."

"Well, now we have a delivery to make. Let's do it so we can move on to the important stuff." She sipped from her mug and grimaced at the lukewarm brew. "And so I can get some Starbucks. Ugh."

———

The autonomous car had to stop at the end of the road. Unfortunately, that wasn't the package's ultimate destination. Ruby climbed out of the driver's side rear seat, and Idryll, back in tiger-woman form, got out of the other side. The trunk popped in response to a tap on her smartphone, and she retrieved the square cardboard box from inside. It was big enough and heavy enough to be awkward, but not enough of either to block her vision or otherwise cause trouble.

The monks had positioned a package receptacle at the bottom of the long sidewalk-slash-staircase that wound up the mountainside to the abbey, but of course, that wasn't adequate to Daphne's needs. *No, apparently if there's a mountain involved, I'm destined to climb it.* The heat prohibited hooded sweatshirts, so she couldn't use magic to make it easier without risking her disguise. She would have asked Idryll to do it since the tiger-woman was doubtless both stronger and more agile than she was, but her partner's mood was iffy since she was also impersonating a human.

She resigned herself to the walk and started up the mountain. Along the way, occasional puffs of mist shot into the air from small sprinklers on either side, cooling them as they climbed. She didn't know much about the Abbey, only that she was looking for Abbot Thomas, presumably the leader of the place, and that they were a bunch of monks who generally didn't interact with the Magic City community except in the form of beer deliveries in both directions. They'd been here before the casinos had gone up when the nearby town was only known as Ely, Nevada and most famous for its railway museum, which probably drew dozens of people from at least a fifty-mile radius a year. *Yes, I'm petty. So what?*

Idryll asked, "Are these people mystics?"

Ruby grunted and shifted the box to a more comfortable position. "They're monks, which is as close as we get to mystics. Not magical but spiritual. Focused on a simple life. Impressive brewers of beer through the ages. I've had some from this one, and it's really good."

"What do you think is in the box?"

She shrugged. "I have no idea. Daphne didn't tell me, and it seemed rude to ask."

They continued the small talk until they rounded a curve and caught sight of the abbey. It was two stories high, constructed of stone, brick, and wood. The exterior was simple, brown and grey depending on the material in question, with windows all the way around. A second building was attached to it, more modern-looking and built of uniform bricks, which was doubtless their brewery. They had four or five brews available at a time but didn't sell them out of the abbey itself, only through establishments in town. She'd had both drafts and bottles and thought that the former was far better than the latter. *Not that I'd turn down a cold one in any container right now.*

As they reached the top, a young man in a grey robe tied with a white rope opened the door to greet them. His smile made him seem even more youthful. His face was nondescript, other than the eager grin, and he seemed a little thin in the big robe. He took the box easily though, suggesting that some muscle hid within. She said, "Thanks, that's from Daphne."

He nodded. "We were expecting this. Thank you for delivering it. Would you like to come in?"

She asked, "Are you Abbot Thomas?" at the same moment that Idryll replied, "We'd love to," and pushed past her into the building. Ruby followed with a sigh, but the truth was, she was curious as well. The entryway was a small room with doors on each side, and he led them first to the one on the right, which turned out to be a storeroom full of shelves.

He slid the box onto one marked, "Food," then explained, "Sometimes people visit us in times of need. We try to have some supplies we can send them off with whenever they're stable and ready to depart. Daphne has been fantastic at collecting clothes, food, and medicines for them."

Ruby replied, "She's always seemed like a good person, but I had no idea she was doing this." *I wish I had because I would've helped her. Well, no reason I can't start doing so.*

"To answer your earlier question, no, I'm not Abbot Thomas. I'm Daniel. I believe the Abbot is over in the brewery if you'd like to meet him."

Idryll replied, "We would," and Ruby nodded agreement.

"Right this way." He proceeded to lead them through a

maze of hallways. They passed other monks along their path, all of whom seemed busy but were more than willing to pause in their efforts to offer a smile and a greeting. She found herself immediately liking all of them and taking comfort in the peacefulness of the surroundings.

"How long have you been here?" she asked as they left the abbey and entered the other building.

"About a year ago, I was thinking about joining the military or going to college, but I decided I needed some time to think about my future before deciding. I'd heard about the abbey from friends who had volunteered their efforts much like Daphne and figured I'd take a look. I've been here ever since." He stopped talking as they reached an older man in a more threadbare robe with snowy hair that fell past his shoulders and a matching close-trimmed beard and mustache. "This is Abbot Thomas."

Ruby introduced herself and her partner and observed, "Pretty impressive place. Are you the brewmaster?"

The older man laughed, and the joy that spilled out of him immediately made all her worries seem lighter. "Well, I'm in charge of the abbey, but when it comes to brewing, I like to think of myself as 'first-taster' rather than brewmaster. I don't know how to do all the things, but I'm pretty clear on what tastes good and what doesn't."

Daniel offered, "They delivered a package from Daphne."

Thomas nodded. "Ah, that woman is a treasure. She's helped us with our efforts to serve the community since she was a little girl. We're very lucky to know her."

Ruby asked, "What sort of efforts?"

He smiled at Daniel. "Thank you. I'll take them from

here." The other man took the dismissal with perfect grace and faded back the way they came. "Daniel is particularly busy today since he's part of the cooking team for the evening meal. To answer your question, we help people in need, any need they may have. Sometimes it's monetary. Sometimes it's food, and sometimes it's a place to stay until they sort something out with their families. Whatever needs doing, we do."

Idryll asked, "So, you're a sanctuary?"

He spread his hands to the sides. "We're a little of everything. Yes, in the classic sense, we would shelter those who are in danger."

Ruby felt the rightness of the place down to her bones and wondered if some magic might be bound up in their commitment to goodwill. *Who knows, maybe the local magical community has added its efforts, with permission or not, to help the abbey along.* She clapped her hands together. "Well, Abbot Thomas, we don't have time to stay right now. I guarantee you'll see more of us in the future. We believe in helping others, too."

CHAPTER TWENTY-TWO

The towering hotel attached to the Ebon Dragon rose in the background of the casino itself, which was several stories high and wrapped in the clutches of its namesake lizard, the chin resting on the roof and the eyes closed as if sleeping. Those eyes opened and looked around at various times of the day, part of a show for the tourists. It was technology, not magic, but worth seeing at least once.

Ruby and Idryll wandered a slow path around the exterior, acquainting themselves with the space while also looking for potential vulnerabilities. They quietly chatted as they did so, but they hadn't come up with anything interesting when they finished the walk. They'd attracted their share of stares, whether because of the tiger-woman's orange, gold, and black mane or because of her white-blond hair, she couldn't tell. Those were the most likely things to draw attention since their clothes were basic and the pair weren't directly interacting with anyone.

Ruby asked, "Seen enough of the outside?"

Idryll nodded. "No clear vulnerabilities out here. I don't sense any hostile magic in use."

She put asking about the extent of that ability on her to-do list and opened the door, waving the other woman inside. Ruby followed her across the threshold and into the interior. The casino had redone it since her last visit. Before, it was meant to look like the dragon's hoard, with gold, silver, and gems on all the surfaces. She'd thought it appropriate but tacky. Of course, sometimes the line between the two was so thin as to be imaginary in casinos. Now, it was all done up in dragon's scales, far more elegant. Some were black, others deep red, and many had a beautiful iridescent sheen. She whistled softly. "Damn, they've made some upgrades. I wonder what my parents think of this." Spirit had long been one of the most fashionable spots on the Magic City Strip, but this would challenge that crown.

They made a slow transit of the interior, Ruby leading the way and running interference as the tiger-woman did whatever it was she did to sense magic. When they'd finished their circuit, they stopped in a small Starbucks café in the casino's restaurant area. She luxuriated in a flat white with a shot of vanilla. Idryll sniffed it, pronounced it "improved but still repulsive," and refused to try it.

"Heathen," Ruby countered and took a deep drink, burning her tongue in the effort to show up her partner. "Damn it to hell." Again, the expression on Idryll's face conveyed the sort of humor that a predator might have watching its prey struggle. "Okay. So, it doesn't look like there's any danger at hand to me. Do you agree?"

The other woman nodded. "Not in this area, anyway."

She was about to ask if they should stay and keep an eye on the place until the time marked on the sheet when a shadow fell across the table. She looked up to find two members of casino security staring down at her. They appeared to be human and wore matching dark suits with dragon pins on the lapels. The jewelry had red eyes, signifying their role at the establishment. Blue was customer assistance, green for dealers and pit bosses, and yellow for management. Every casino had a similar system, and her brain always catalogued it automatically when she encountered it. "Something we can do for you, gentlemen?" Their suits weren't cut well enough to hide the holsters under the jackets. *Probably tasers, but given what happened at the Mist, maybe not.*

They both looked alike, musclebound with short hair and hard eyes. The one on the right, who was notable only because his hair was darker than the other's, nodded. "The casino manager would like a word, Miss Achera."

Outwardly, she nodded and rose. "Lead the way." Inwardly, she cursed her luck. *What the hell am I going to say? "Hey, someone's planning to attack your place, but it's not me, and no, I can't tell you how I know." Why does trying to be helpful have to be so damn difficult?*

She hadn't met the casino manager before, but she knew the type. Rosalind Caruthers was undoubtedly a witch, despite appearing utterly human in her navy business suit and black blouse. The skirt was cut above the knees to reveal strong legs and expensive shoes. Her dragon pin had diamond eyes and was likely unique, given her position. She'd risen from behind the desk in her luxurious office, exchanged handshakes with each of them, and gestured them to a couch that sat across the room by the windows. They were high up in the hotel tower, a corner suite a few floors down from the top.

Caruthers took her seat in a chair at a ninety-degree angle to the couch and accepted a glass of seltzer and ice from an assistant. The assistant then set coasters and additional glasses of the same on the wooden table in front of the seats. "So," the executive asked, "to what do I owe the pleasure of a visit from the Achera family?"

Ruby leaned forward and sipped the drink, which was as delicious and refreshing as one would expect. "I'm not here on behalf of my family or anything. A friend came to town unexpectedly, and I'm showing her around. Of course, I had to bring her to the Ebon Dragon."

"Of course," the witch agreed with a smile that looked the tiniest bit fake on her lips. "Naturally, our security is a little touchy right now, and on the lookout for people who appear to be doing more looking around than gaming."

"Surely you're not suggesting I had something to do with the events at the Mist?"

The fake part of the smile vanished, leaving a real one. "Oh, I'm aware that you had something to do with it, Miss Achera. I've seen the video."

Ruby cringed, waiting for her to reveal something more, but nothing came. "Well then, you certainly can't believe I had anything to do with the bastards who tried to rob the place."

"Nor those who tried to blow it up, I would imagine.

Yet here you are, checking out my casino only a couple of days later."

Idryll interjected, "It's quite beautiful. I was glad to have a tour of it."

Caruthers's gaze swiveled toward the other woman, and she offered thanks for the compliment. Then she asked, "Where are you from?"

The tiger-woman laughed. "Somewhere far from here. New York." It's what Ruby had told her to answer if the question ever came up, and she was pleased to see her advice followed.

The executive's eyes shifted back to Ruby, then to her assistant as the door to the suite opened. She nodded. "I'm only the appetizer for this meeting, so I'll take my leave. It was wonderful to meet both of you. If you decide to visit the Ebon Dragon again, please make yourselves known to any of the staff, and I'll stake you at the tables."

She rose and left without waiting for their answer, exchanging nods with a man in a grey suit, white shirt, and dark blue tie. He took the chair she'd vacated but didn't relax into it. He sat on the edge with a rigid spine and a serious expression. "Miss Ruby Achera. Who's your friend?"

The imperious attitude coming off the man set her immediately at odds with him. "Her name's Idryll. Who the hell are you?"

He offered a thin smile and dipped his hand into an inside pocket, and pulled out an identification card that read "Paul Andrews, Paranormal Defense Agency." She handed it back. "Reno or Vegas?"

"Reno."

"Ah. I'm sorry. Must be a pain being the little office all the time."

He chuckled without mirth. "You'd be surprised. A lot of scumbags think the rest of Nevada is a safe place to operate." His eyes didn't leave hers.

She sipped her seltzer, delaying long enough to be sure he knew that she was doing it to be annoying, then set it down. "Are you suggesting I'm one of those scumbags, Agent Andrews? You're aware of who I am, which should make such a thing obviously ludicrous."

He shrugged. "It's astonishing what some people will do for money, right up to and including trying to take out the competition with more direct means than simple business tactics."

Ruby chuckled. "All's fair in love, war, and business, is that what you think? Sorry to disappoint you, but the family's doing fine, Spirit is doing fine, and we had neither motive nor opportunity to pull off the action at the Mist."

"But you most certainly had the means. You have a degree in magical engineering, correct?"

"I do. I heard a rumor the explosive devices were partially magical. However, I assure you that even if I wanted to do such a thing, which I don't, I have zero experience with that sort of combination. You can feel free to check with my professors on that score."

He nodded. "We already did. Still, who knows? You might have been freelancing on the side, building up your skills."

Ruby sighed. "Now you're fishing. While this conversation has been nothing short of *delightful*, Agent, unless you have a piece of paper to show that gives you the right to detain us, my friend and I have other casinos to visit."

"To scout out, you mean."

She stood, and he did too, a little too fast for comfort. *Probably a physical intimidation trick he picked up somewhere. Wonder how he'd react to a kick in the crotch.* She stared into his eyes, making sure he saw that she wasn't impressed. "You can use whatever words you like. It doesn't change the fact that we've done nothing against the law and aren't going to do anything against the law. Perhaps you should spend your time looking for the real culprits."

"I have plenty of time Miss Achera, to be sure I take a good long look at *anyone* who might be involved."

She walked toward the door while pulling Idryll along with her by the arm. "Enjoy your time in Magic City, Agent."

The encounter had left Ruby shaky, and she found a seat out in the sun where she and Idryll could talk. The number of tourists wandering the Strip wasn't near Vegas numbers, but there were a lot of them, mostly magical. She wished for some sort of James Bond communication earpiece so they could chat without being seen talking and made a mental note to discuss it with Margrave. She ventured, "I'm concerned."

Idryll nodded. "If I were you, I would be about a great many things. To which do you refer?"

"Being noticed. I don't like the idea that my actions could blow back on my family."

"Or your roommates."

A trill of fear rippled through her. "Yeah, them too. Or you, although you can take care of yourself against most threats."

She nodded and hissed softly at a dog being walked along the opposite side of the large thoroughfare. "What is this Paranormal Defense Agency?" She said the words as though they were quite foreign to her.

"A government department that watches out for magical threats."

"He thinks you're one? And didn't notice that I *am* one? That one is not very good at his job."

Ruby couldn't help but laugh. "They're thinking of threats on a larger scale. What happened at the Mist wouldn't normally be big enough to draw their attention." She paused as the pieces fell into place. "Which means they think it's part of something bigger, too. Something *magical*. That kind of argues against the security companies, since the ones here are all run by humans, as far as I know."

Idryll shrugged. "It seems as if the only way to figure it out is to be here tonight at two-two-zero-zero."

"Twenty-two-hundred," she corrected automatically. "We're missing something here. I can feel it. Let's go back to my parents' place, have a nap, and think it over. I agree. Tonight we have to be here, and between now and then we also have to figure out how to make sure that Agent Andrews doesn't know we've returned."

CHAPTER TWENTY-THREE

They'd dropped through the shaft in the back of the nearest casino, which Idryll had loved. Ruby had used her magic to cushion the other's descent, but the tiger-woman assured her that now that she knew how it worked, she'd be able to handle it on her own from then on. She shrank to her Bengal form, and Ruby rigged a sling with the clothes she'd worn to keep her hands free. *No way would a self-respecting cat walk through the kemana like some common creature.*

Matthias greeted them and delivered a bowl of chicken and another of water to her room shortly after they got up there. The cat dove greedily into the food while Ruby snuggled under the covers, sternly promising her brain that if it didn't figure some stuff out while she was asleep, there would be trouble between them.

Miracle of miracles, she had identified some paths forward when she woke up a couple of hours later. She slapped the off button on the old-school windup alarm clock, which she depended on because only magically assisted technology would function in the kemana, and that not completely reliably. She resisted petting Idryll, who slept on the bed in cat form, then went and took a decadent shower, washing and conditioning her hair twice before turning the showerhead to massage and standing under the pounding flow of water for as long as she could stand it.

Ruby came out, dressed quickly, and pointed at the cat. "I have to go through some boxes. Staying here or coming with?" Idryll yawned, stretched, and rolled over to face the wall, providing her answer quite clearly. "Fine. Be that way." *I'll go into the spooky attic by myself. Thanks for nothing, "partner."*

In truth, the attic was entirely unexciting. It was clean and well-organized and only a little colder than the rest of the house. Staying warm was sometimes a challenge in the underground city since many people used individual magic to keep themselves toasty, and she generally couldn't. Here, with no one to see her, she let her disguise fade and wrapped herself in a force shield filled with air warmed by a very gentle application of fire magic.

She walked through the stacked plastic crates until she spotted the one she sought. One of her favorite holidays, and one of the most popular in the kemana, was Halloween. Since she was allegedly human, physical costumes had been required, rather than illusion. At the time it had been annoying, but she'd gotten good at doing makeup, both subtle and dramatic, which had made her a hit during Halloween parties at the university. *It has to be here somewhere.* She dug through costumes until she found what she was looking for, part of an outfit she'd worn as a teenager. It was a Catwoman mask from the Michelle Pfeiffer movie, black with white stitching. It covered more of the face than the film version but left the eyes, mouth, and chin free. Most importantly, it covered her hair and ears, which would permit her to use magic without giving away her secret.

She took her treasure back to the bedroom and showed it to Idryll. The cat yawned, rolled over, and went to sleep, clearly unimpressed. "Yeah, whatever, you suck. Now, let's see what else I can come up with so no one recognizes me tonight."

She would have to be satisfied with what was readily available, knowing that if tonight didn't give her the answers she needed, she'd have to figure out something better. There wasn't time to do it now. All that mattered was that if anyone saw her, no one connected the woman in the mask to Ruby Achera. She picked up the black tactical pants she'd worn at the security company and set them aside. *No, they might make that connection. So, no tactical pants and no hooded sweatshirt. What, then?* She strode into the walk-in closet that held clothes she hadn't taken to school with her the past year. She spotted a good option immediately, an outfit she'd bought for a club night party. Black leather pants, a thick-link silver chain belt, and the tight long-sleeved tunic would hide her tattoos. She took the items back into the bedroom and shoved them in a bag so no one would see her with them in the house.

Needs one more thing, though. I can't wear mine, because

people have seen me in it. She crept down the hall to her sister's room and put her ear to the door. Hearing nothing, she snuck inside and invaded her closet. She remembered a particular jacket that she'd loved and pawed through Morrigan's clothes until she found it. It was bright red leather, thigh-length, with an offset zipper that went all the way up to the standing collar. It wouldn't be subtle, but it was also something that Ruby would never think of wearing, normally. Since her sister would have an alibi, no one could accuse her if someone recognized it. *Win-win-win. Jackpot.*

The next question was how to deal with the situation at the Ebon Dragon. They couldn't lurk around the place, even with a veil. The establishment was sure to have magical security in addition to the mundane kind, as her family did. However, a train of thought had kicked off with the mask's discovery and a remembrance of how Five pushed Selina Kyle out the window of a tall building. Height was the key. If they could get to the top of the hotel part of the casino unseen, they could look out for trouble from up there. If she were lucky, they'd have a way to watch from the inside, as well.

She grabbed the snoring Idryll and created a portal to the garage near the house she shared with her roommates. She rushed in, dumped the cat on the bed, then texted Demetrius to see if he was free. He told her he'd be good in an hour, so she used the time to make some food for herself and Idryll, who took it as a peace offering while refusing to talk to her. Ruby observed, "You know, silence is nice. I could get used to this." The cat glared at her but didn't rise to the bait.

At the appointed time, she went down to the dining room and found him waiting. She asked, "Do I correctly remember you saying you'd done a job for the folks at the Ebon Dragon?"

He nodded. "Lots of them. I worked there before I went out on my own. Why?" Suspicion colored his question.

"I need a favor, and I need you to trust me on this."

"Is it going to get me into trouble?"

She sighed. "I wish I could say absolutely not, but I guess there's always a possibility. Depends on how good you are and on how bad things go."

He grinned. "Oh, I'm very good. What bad things are you thinking of?"

Ruby drummed her fingers on the table. "I think you'd be better off not knowing. In case of the bad things."

Demetrius shook his head. "No way. One thing you learn right off the bat in the infomancy business is that you don't do blind jobs. Tell me what's up, or no dice. Not even for a roommate."

Damn and double damn. She was deliberately trying to limit the risk to others, but here she was about to put her roommate directly into the middle of her plans. *Yet, there's no way around it if I'm going to have eyes inside and outside.* "Okay. I'm only telling you the minor details."

He shrugged. "Tell me what you can, and we'll see if it's enough." She sensed a slight distance that hadn't been there before. It caused a twinge somewhere near her heart, but she pressed on.

"Okay. Here's the thing. I got a tip that something bad is going down at the Ebon Dragon tonight. I don't want to share the source," *since it involves criminal activity*, she tacked on mentally, "but I have great faith in this information's reliability."

"Continue." He'd closed his eyes and seemed to be concentrating all his attention on listening.

"I can only keep watch on the outside or the inside. I figure security's going to be lighter on the outside, so I'll put my focus there. I still need a way to be sure that nothing weird is going on inside. The best way I know to do that would be access to the cameras."

He sighed. "That's so illegal."

Ruby spread her hands wide on the table. "Yeah, I know. I don't have anything else I can do."

"Maybe warn the casino? Warn the police?"

She scratched the back of her neck, which itched like someone was using it as a target. "Yeah, about that. I was in there today trying to be sure that no one had planted explosives, and I got what you might call a frosty welcome."

"Casino security?"

"The manager. Plus some dude from the Reno PDA."

Demetrius sat straighter at that revelation. "Shit. Really?"

Ruby nodded. "Really, really. That's why if something happens there tonight, I'm screwed whether I'm there or not. They'll try to blame me no matter what the truth is.

On Caruthers' part, causing chaos for the owners of another casino is a win in itself."

He shook his head. "Okay. I get it. What do you plan to do if you see something?"

"Depends on what it is. If it's small enough, I'll stop it. If it's not, I'll call in a tip and be sure to show up somewhere so I can have an alibi."

"This is stupid."

She laughed darkly. "I know. I don't have a better idea. Do you?"

He paused for almost a full minute, and she could tell that he was thinking furiously about the problem. Finally, he sighed and confirmed, "No, I don't. Here's what I'll do. I can probably get into the system and see the cameras with a reasonable deniability level by putting a work order into their lower-security billing system. There's no way I'll be able to do more than view it, and I certainly don't want to be seen sending it anywhere."

"So, what does that mean?"

He grinned. "It means I'm your guy in the chair."

Ruby frowned. "What?"

Demetrius rolled his eyes. "Are you telling me that you didn't see *Spider-Man: Homecoming*? I'm losing a hell of a lot of respect for you right now, Ruby. The guy in the chair, who helps out the person in the field."

"Ahh, gotcha. Yes, good. How will we communicate?"

"Burner phones. If you tell me that you don't know what they are, I'm done with you."

She laughed. "I've seen all the Jason Bourne movies. I know what you mean."

"Good. Then go get some, and I'll see about organizing this."

She returned to her room and told Idryll, "Going out. Back soon. Buying phones."

The cat looked at her like she was crazy. *Yeah, kitty, you could be right. Except if I'm crazy, why do I feel so good about doing this?*

CHAPTER TWENTY-FOUR

The burner phone rested in Ruby's pocket, its twin safely back at the house with Demetrius. She wouldn't connect to him until she was in position. Her plan to accomplish that had seemed reasonable when she'd come up with it earlier, but now, standing on the roof of the hotel that served Spirit's casino, she thought maybe she'd been a little optimistic.

Or, as Idryll had observed, "Incredibly stupid." She'd followed that observation up with an equally judgmental question. "Do you have a death wish?"

Ruby had snapped, "Only if it involves yours," and stomped off. They'd portaled to the office, then made their way into the hotel area. She had access to anywhere in the facility by virtue of the Owner's Key, a credit card-sized credential that would unlock any door and control any elevator. In this case it was the freight lift, which had carried them up to the top of the tall structure. Her partner had hidden in her backpack in a kitten version of the Bengal, seemingly thoroughly disgruntled about doing so.

The first order of business now that Idryll had dashed around to confirm they were alone was to change into her costume. The wind at this elevation blew a chill night breeze, and she shivered as she slipped on the leather pants and the boots, then tucked in the tunic, making sure to pull it down over her wrists. *If I replace this sometime, I'll need to add something to keep it in position, like a finger loop, maybe.* The chain belt went next, then the red leather jacket. The final clothing item had a few pockets. She stuffed several potentially useful toys into them before pushing the backpack into a corner beside some equipment, where it should be safe until she could retrieve it.

She tugged on her mask and made sure to properly tuck any loose strands of her hair underneath so they couldn't give her away. Then she tossed one of the other Halloween costumes she'd brought to Idryll, who hissed at it and let it drop to the roof. The tiger-woman said, "I will not."

Ruby shrugged. "If you're coming with me, you have to. We can't risk anyone seeing you. Besides, it's a catsuit. *Cat* suit. Get it? It's perfect." It was Emma Peel's version from the non-Marvel Avengers, with the black mask of one of her brother's superhero costumes from long before.

"Anyone who sees me, I'll simply kill. Problem solved."

She snorted. "In an age of cell phones, drones, surveillance, and who knows what else, we can't rely on that. Plus, you know, they put people in jail forever for that sort of thing." In a more serious tone, she coaxed, "Idryll, please. We'll find a better way later. It's twenty minutes until the time they set. We can't delay."

The tiger woman growled as she bent to pick up the outfit. "You owe me for this. Big."

"Biggest ball of yarn ever. Promise." The look she received in return for that comment convinced her it was time to stop needling the shapeshifter. Instead, she walked to the edge of the roof and looked down at the top of the Ebon Dragon's hotel, about three hundred feet away and fifteen stories down, and the wizards' and witches' casino many stories below that. *This would be so much easier if I didn't suck at portals.* Ruby wasn't particularly afraid of heights, but she couldn't claim to be comfortable looking at the potential drop if she screwed up.

So don't screw up. She built up the picture in her mind, saw the object materialize, and imagined them using it to cross the intervening space to the other building. Once they got there, they'd connect with Demetrius, who was hopefully watching the interior by now.

Her partner stepped beside her and looked down, then shook her head. "Are you sure you want to do this? Is it so important to you?"

Ruby had asked herself that a dozen times already in the last hour, and the answer always came up the same. "It's important for *everyone*. The bad people can't hurt innocents and get away with it. If the good people of the city don't stand against it, who will? If no one does, what then? Law of the Jungle? Hell no, not in my town."

Idryll shrugged. "Well, I'm in your stupid costume. Let's do it then."

A glance over showed her that the tiger-woman was indeed dressed and looked way better in the catsuit than

Ruby had when she'd worn it. *Jerk.* "Okay. Here goes." She summoned her magic, let it build inside her until she had enough of it to extend the bridge at least halfway across, then released it. A semicircular tube of force reached out, angling down toward the roof of the Ebon Dragon's hotel. Unlike blasts of magic or simple spells, she would have to hold this one and add to it, which required her to keep it fixed in her mind.

Before she could think about it too much, she jumped in and started to slide. She kept her eyes on the end of it, adding more length to the tube as they slid, increasing the pace as their speed built. Behind her, Idryll shouted with excitement, something between a roar and a "whee!" *This would be fun if not for the need to keep it from vanishing underneath us.* The idea made their support wobble a little, and she quickly snapped her brain back to proper focus.

They rocketed forward faster than she'd anticipated, but she didn't have the bandwidth to do anything except add a gentle curve into the route. Not enough to throw them off the edge but enough to induce some drag on their momentum. It wasn't until they were only forty feet away that she saw the figures on the roof. They were dressed in black and numbered at least a dozen. The first ones went over the edge while she watched, apparently on ropes by the way they moved.

She turned her head to warn her partner, but the tiger-woman said, "I see them. Get us to the roof. We can deal with them after." Ruby whispered a small prayer to the universe that no one would look in their direction and see her bright red coat sliding through the air toward them. She'd aimed the slide at the point where they'd have the greatest distance to stop before smashing into anything, which lay on the opposite side of the surface from where the black-suited figures dropped over the edge.

Ruby called, "They're probably going down for the casino roof from there. Weird as it is, it might be easier to stay hidden that way than if they'd tried to go up from the ground." She estimated they faced mainly or entirely non-magicals since a magical could probably veil and make it up to the casino roof from ground level with ease. *Well, that's one advantage, I guess.* Her boots failed to find purchase as she hit the gravel-and-tar surface, and she let herself fall into a slide. Idryll, on the other hand, found her balance immediately and moved to attack.

The trip down the magical slide had been exhilarating for multiple reasons. First, obviously, because it was fast and fun and a little dangerous. Second, and more importantly, because it showed that her new Mist Elf partner had power. It wasn't a novice trick to accomplish something on that scale, and even less so to do it while using it. She'd seen a glimmer of that talent in the security company break-in, but this was far more.

Of course, she'd had enough faith to trust her life to that talent, so survival alone might be part of what made her feel so great at the moment. She had enemies to deal with in any case and didn't intend to be as gentle with them as she had the others. She had no doubt that these people were up to no good and hoped Ruby saw it, too.

Seven individuals stood on the roof. Two were separated from the rest, off by a piece of metallic equipment that dwarfed them both. She'd leave them to her partner. The rest appeared to be preparing to descend or helping others to do so, or whatever. Her first leap had given her a good view of the situation before another giant hunk of metal that did who-knew-what interposed itself in her vision. She hit the roof and leapt again, this time at a slightly changed angle. It would throw off their aim if she'd been spotted and also land her behind the ones farther from the edge.

They saw her as she cleared the obstacle, and shots rang out. She twisted in mid-air to avoid the attacks and landed perfectly balanced behind one of the men, who was only halfway through his turn toward where he'd anticipated she'd land. She lashed out in a kick that propelled him forward, smashing him into one nearer to the edge and sending them both over, locked in one another's arms. A scream abruptly cut off as she went after the other three.

She slithered in, staying low and shifting from side to side to hinder their aim. Bullets slapped off the surrounding surface, and one grazed her arm, ripping through the thin costume and drawing blood. Idryll snarled as she lashed out at the one who had shot her, retracting the claws that had reflexively extended before her hand impacted his face. The punch was strong enough to flip him around as he fell, twining him in the line that she now saw ran through some sort of attachment on a harness he wore. The two that remained shot at her a few more times, but she was already diving away into a hand-spring that would bring her to the one on the right. She'd intended to kick him, but instead of taking the blow, he simply jumped backward off the roof.

The other man lifted his gun with a confident smile full of malice, and she knew she had no chance of reaching him before he shot her. So, she did the only thing she could, and leapt off the roof as well.

CHAPTER TWENTY-FIVE

Ruby closed the distance to her duo at a fast shuffle. They hadn't seen her and appeared to be intent on whatever task they had in mind. A *clank* accompanied the removal of a large grate, and the opening beyond was clearly part of the building's HVAC system. She'd had to learn how facilities operated for the family business and recognized the unit as identical to the ones on Spirit's roof.

She wondered if they'd be stupid enough to crawl into the ductwork, like in the movies, but instead they threaded a hose down into it, and fear shot through her. *Some kind of poison gas into the hotel? Or maybe explosives? That's...insane.* Ruby had wrapped her mind around the idea that, for business reasons, a little collateral damage like the lives lost at the Mist might make sense in someone's demented imagination. But she couldn't, just *couldn't*, imagine what would make whatever this pair might be up to okay.

Her instinct was to blast them with force or fire, but both of those were pretty high on the lethal scale. She grabbed one of the globes Margrave had created for her, which had sound, light, and smoke all contained within a glass shell and hurled it at their feet. It went off, causing them both to shout, flinch away, and most importantly, drop what they were doing. She channeled her rush forward into a stiff arm that slammed into the back of the first one's head, ramming him face-first into the aluminum side of the HVAC vent. It buckled, which probably saved the man from having all the bones in his skull broken.

The second one was quick, going for a gun in a shoulder holster at her appearance. He managed to free it before her crescent kick smashed it out of his hand and down the HVAC shaft. The move left him wide open, a veritable buffet of attack points, but she was in a hurry. She snapped a foot up into his groin and rammed an uprising knee into his face as he buckled from the first strike. He went down, moaning. Ruby caught motion in her peripheral vision and suppressed a scream as Idryll dropped over the edge. *She did it on purpose. I'm sure she has a reason. She's a cat. She can probably magically fall from whatever height and still land on her feet.*

She bent to the metal canisters lying on the rooftop with hoses attached, both of which had several hazard stickers on them. *Damn it. What the hell am I supposed to do with these?* She couldn't leave them and the two men up here for fear of what they might do but also wanted to be sure the evidence remained with them. *Damn, damn, damn.* She stalked the roof, looking for options. Ultimately, the best she could come up with was to take off her chain belt and use it to bind the men's hands behind them and to one another, then loop it around one of the many pipes that stuck out of the roof. A focused application of fire magic melted it into place. *Hopefully, that'll hold.* She flipped open the burner phone and dialed.

"Go," Demetrius answered.

"Anything inside?" Ruby walked toward the edge.

"Nothing."

"Okay, we have stuff outside. Call nine-one-one and get them to the hotel roof immediately. Hell, have them evacuate the place if they can, maybe. Mention terrorists and hazmat." She was positive he'd have a way to notify the police that didn't include giving them his identity or location. *Otherwise, what's infomancy for, anyway?*

"Got it."

"Call if anything happens inside." She clicked off the phone and shoved it back in a pocket, then looked down over the edge. Men ran around on the roof of the casino itself, more slid down the lines, and two hung upside-down near the top, holding on to one another for dear life. Ruby couldn't help but laugh. Farther down, she spotted Idryll sliding down one of the ropes after the rest and grinned. *All right. Now we're talking.*

Ruby jumped off the edge.

———

Idryll slid down the cable as fast as it would carry her, thankful for the costume that protected her paws. Her keen eyesight picked out the activity on the casino roof with ease. Men moved around and pulled what looked like large metal containers out of dark bags. When she'd hopped over the side, she'd had a vision of careening down the rope and knocking the black-suited people off it along the way, but they, too, moved as fast as they could. It appeared she wouldn't catch any before the ride was over.

That's fine. I'll be in time to mess with whatever they've planned. The enemies awaiting her below arranged themselves in anticipation of her arrival. Four of them spread into a semicircle around the end of the rope while the others went to assist the ones that were doing, well, whatever they were doing. She squeezed harder on the line to slow her drop enough that she could control her footing when she reached the bottom.

When she was about fifty feet from them, shots rang out and utterly failed to hit her. The crowd she saw around the edges of the casino building scattered in response to the gunfire, which was likely good for their safety but probably not a useful contribution to Ruby's ability to escape the situation unseen. *One problem at a time.* Fortunately, the criminals below weren't doing a very good job of hitting her as she varied her speed by gripping and releasing the line. When she was twenty-five feet up or so, she released the cable and dropped.

In her pure tiger form, she could drop from a much greater height without injury. It was part of her inborn magic. It carried into this form, but at a reduced level. When she landed she dove and rolled, somersaulting twice before gathering her feet under her and driving forward in a running tackle at the nearest. He went down under her unexpected charge, and the gunfire stopped, the men unwilling to risk hitting one another in the crossfire she'd created. Her knees came down on his ribs, and the sound of his bones cracking was audible even through the armor he wore.

She dove forward in another somersault, assuming the others would attack from behind, and came up in a spin. Sure enough, they were advancing, each of them holding one of the sparking sticks she'd faced before. She grinned. "Do you think your little twigs will bother me, cowards?" The most aggressive of them stepped toward her in response, and she feinted at him, the speed of her move causing him to stumble backward in alarm. She laughed mockingly as she attacked the other pair.

Foolishly, they both used the same dominant hand, meaning that the one on her right couldn't risk a full swing without hitting his partner. She ran at the center of them and slid to the right, whipping her feet around in a sweep that took that one to the ground. Idryll lacked time to finish him since the other engaged quickly and jabbed the tip of the weapon at her. She batted it aside, careful not to touch the end, then stomped on the downed man's chest as she attacked the other. He got a hand up to block her first swing at his head and interposed the baton to knock her jab at his solar plexus off-target. Nothing stopped her knee from driving into his groin. She twisted to take control of the wrist that held the electrical baton and drove it down into the fallen man as the one she restrained crumpled behind her.

Then only the third one remained. She slowly stalked toward him until Ruby appeared and snatched her prey away.

As she dropped, far faster than she'd ever allowed herself to do before, Ruby took stock of the scene below. Idryll had one of the three groups under control, but the others concerned her—the ones that were busy with canisters she recognized from up above. *It's lucky we arrived early. Hell, it's fortunate we figured it out at all.* She wasn't sure what was in the silver containers, but she was quite confident it wasn't something that would be good for anyone who breathed it.

She used a blast of force magic to slow her at the end and landed already in motion toward her foes. If she'd had more confidence or more practice, she probably could have used the building's surface to push her farther, to glide a little better. *A challenge for another day, maybe.* She was running at full speed when she came up behind Idryll's last opponent and smashed an elbow into the back of his head as she passed.

Ahead, two separate groups worked with the canisters at different locations, about twenty feet apart. She grabbed the last globe from her pocket and threw it at the group on the right, then diverted toward the ones on the left. It detonated before she got there, alerting everyone to her presence, so they were up and ready to greet her when she arrived.

Not that it helped them. *After all those different martial arts, one would hope I would be reasonably good by now.* One had drawn a baton, and the other had gone for his pistol, which earned him the position of most immediate threat. She wished she had her knives or something blunt to throw at him, but all she had was herself. *Keshalla won't be pleased. I'll plan better next time.* The gun was in the man's right hand, so she went low and to the left, flicking her fingers to create a force burst. His weapon flew away, and he'd been so focused on offense that he'd left himself open to attack. She stepped past him with her right foot and pistoned her knee into the middle of his torso.

He crumpled forward, and she put her hands on his shoulder and hip and pushed, adding a force blast from each hand to the thrust. He flew into the air and collided with his partner, and they both tumbled toward the low wall that ran around the edge of the roof. Ruby spun to the last ones as Idryll got to them. The tiger-woman made short work of the pair, and it was over.

Except for the sirens and police cars and loudspeakers coming from below. "Damn it." She ran for the ropes and used them to climb to the lowest hotel room window, which she shattered with a force blast. Idryll followed her through the room, and Ruby led her on a race through the hallway, figuring out the hotel's arrangement in her mind. It was an L-shape like most of them, and she needed to get out of sight of the front. They made a left at the end, and she blasted the handle off a door with a ball of force at a downward angle, in case anyone was in the room.

It was empty, and again she broke the window with her magic. It was three stories to the ground. Idryll swung out and climbed down the side of the building. Ruby jumped and used force magic to cushion her fall. She met up with the other woman and cast three spells—a disguise for each of them and a veil that would render them invisible. That way, if someone made it through the first defense, they'd look like girlfriends out for a night on the town.

Idryll said, "We did well. Except, how did you know?"

Ruby frowned. "How did I know what?"

"How did you know that the anti-magic emitters in the casino wouldn't reach high enough to cancel your magic when you fell?"

Her stomach fell at the realization that she'd never considered it. She cleared her throat and choked out, "Instinct."

The tiger-woman laughed. "Perhaps best not to rely totally on instinct in the future, despite your obvious ability."

Yeah. Perhaps.

CHAPTER TWENTY-SIX

Jared Trenton hadn't been able to help himself. Although he needed to stay unconnected to the event, he wanted to be a part of it. He'd been in an outdoor restaurant across the Strip from the Ebon Dragon at the appointed hour, along with a random date he'd met online for cover. The meal had been good, the company better, but then the only thing that could have ruined his night, did. When he heard the first siren shortly before ten o'clock, he knew that something had gone wrong. When the motorcycles drove down the middle of the thoroughfare with their lights flashing, it was clear that it had gone *really* wrong.

With a skill he'd developed in the military, he put the worry into a small box in his mind to ignore until he was ready for it. He continued to charm his date, took her for an after-dinner drink, then apologized at her door for having to end the evening early because of work. He had her number and might call her again. *Assuming I survive long enough to do it.*

He texted Grentham and arranged a meeting, then

drove to the bar the dwarf had selected. The space was dark with flickering candles in red jars on the tables and comfortably over-padded chairs. Wood paneling covered the walls with antique rifles as decoration, each with a nameplate. It was called The Armory, naturally, and was located a few blocks off the Strip, far enough to discourage the tourists from wandering in.

No servers were present. You ordered, picked up, and paid by the drink at the bar. They wouldn't run a tab, but they would set up an account for you to draw from if you visited often enough. Both he and Grentham had one and alternated picking up the rounds. The dwarf returned from the bar with two tumblers of Scotch whiskey, doubles both, with a single round ice cube in each. He carefully placed one before Jared and sat across from him. The surrounding noise was sufficient to keep their conversation private as long as they didn't shout at each other and as long as no one actively listened in. He checked his smartphone, which had tech that would pick up microphones, and saw none. He trusted his partner would have done the same for magical means of eaves-dropping.

Jared leaned forward. "What the hell happened? Did you hear from them?"

The dwarf sipped his drink, winced, and set it on the table in front of him. "No. I was watching. Someone came in and blew up the op. Two of 'em. At least one was a magical."

"How do you know?"

Grentham's lips twisted in a snarl. "Because they did damn magic, how the hell do you think?" He raised a hand as soon as he finished. "I'm sorry. I'm so damned angry that I wasn't there to take them out."

Jared understood that feeling well. He'd had the same reaction to the two that broke into the security building. *Two.* "What are the odds that we'd have two different pairs of people suddenly messing around in our business on two separate occasions?"

His tablemate pulled his dark beard, one of the things he did when he was agitated. "I'd say about a thousand to one, at best. It has to be the same pair. That means they found something at the headquarters that led them there. This means that *someone* is going to get their ass kicked when I find out who's not employing proper information discipline."

"The next question is, who are these two, and who's aiming them at us? Maybe they work for our competition?"

"I don't think so. At least not a normal crew. We do a pretty good job of keeping an eye on them all. It could be that one of them hired specialists."

He took a mouthful of the Scotch and savored it for several seconds before letting it trickle down his throat. "Regardless, we need to take them out before they do any more damage to us. Do we have exposure from the last op?"

The other man shook his head. "No chance. Our people were only involved in planning, hiring, and delivering the material. The rest were all freelancers. If any survived, they have nothing to give to the cops."

Jared chuckled. "If they did, we'd know it right away, anyway." He had contacts in the Ely Police Department who were still well-paid to throw useful pieces of information his way. As long as he had a company, he'd maintain *that* cash flow. *Not least because it's the one that will give me the warning to get out of town if it all goes to hell.* "So, I didn't want to distract you with this until the current job was over, but we have new orders. They're intense."

For the first time that evening, the dwarf's expression approached a smile. "Oh, really? Do tell."

Ruby and Idryll had wandered most of the way down the Strip underneath the veil before dropping it and portaling first to the roof of Spirit to collect the backpack she'd left behind, then to her bedroom in her family's home. The tiger-woman had discarded the catsuit and collapsed on the bed immediately, while Ruby shoved their costumes into a bag. She opened a portal into her *other* bedroom, threw the bag through, and marched off to the shower now that she'd hidden the evidence of their escapade. *More or less. One hopes that my roomies aren't hanging out in my room when I'm not there.*

When she woke up the next morning, she headed for the kitchen. Matthias was there, eating breakfast at a small table in the corner that the staff used for meals. Ruby yawned and poured herself a mug of coffee. "Dang, it's early. Do you always get up before the sun?"

He laughed and gestured at the seat across from him, which she took gratefully. No family member would think of assuming an invitation to that table; it just wasn't done. "Indeed. One has to be ready for the earliest riser.

However, I didn't anticipate quite how early that would be, in your case."

She waved a hand to dismiss the concern. "I don't need any assistance. Only this coffee and maybe a couple of those muffins." He passed the covered basket to her, and she discovered that her nose had been right: both blueberry and raspberry varieties lay within, likely left in the oven the night before on a timer so they'd be fresh in the morning. She broke them in half, gave each a light sheen of butter, and took a bite of the raspberry muffin, which was the perfect blend of tart and sweet. "Oh, I'm in heaven."

She'd shared an early morning with Matthias on any number of occasions in the past and was pleased to see that he continued his habit of reading the newspaper during the meal. The *Magic City Gazette* still printed a daily paper, thanks to the abundant advertising aimed mainly at the tourists. Every hotel provided copies for its guests, and each of the Mist Elf casinos dropped a bundle down to the kemana. He was reading the second section, so she reached across and grabbed the first.

The events at the Ebon Dragon covered the front page. It focused on the police response in answer to an anonymous tip and said that they'd taken the perpetrators to jail. Having been caught in the act, they were likely to receive multi-year sentences since the canisters contained a poisonous substance. If it had gotten into the air vents, it likely would have resulted in several deaths. The article discussed the dangerous chemical, and Ruby's frown grew with each paragraph she read. The poison wasn't strong enough to kill everyone in there, not dispersed like that. *If they weren't trying to kill all the guests, the question again is what the hell were they trying to do? Sure, some people probably would have died, but the rest would have gotten sick. Like the Mist, this looks like one thing disguised as another. In this case, terrorism instead of a robbery.*

She set the paper down with a sigh and went back to eating her muffins in silence while her brain churned on the question. Matthias inquired, "What do you think of the excitement at the Ebon Dragon?"

Ruby put on her casino owner hat as she considered how to respond. "Obviously, casinos are being targeted. I might have worried that it was directed at Mist Elves for some reason, but now that's proven false. I can't help but think there's a big picture here."

Her breakfast companion nodded. "Sowing division above, perhaps to do the same below?"

Her brain skidded to a screeching halt. "I didn't consider that. Surely the council wouldn't find itself threatened by this."

"It could go either way. A closer bond in the face of a common challenge, or suspicion that one among them is behind it."

From bad to worse. I need to figure this out. "Have you discussed this with my parents?"

"One is sure they're already aware, Miss Ruby."

"Yeah, of course, they would be. If I want to avoid having to see Dralen, I better get a move on."

She exited to the sound of Matthias' laughter. When she got back to her room, her partner was awake and stared at her with an expectant expression. Ruby waited for a second, and when she didn't talk, asked, "What?"

"It is time to go hunting."

"Come again?"

The cat bared her teeth. "I recognized a scent last night. One of those men had been around the magic at the security company or had been near someone who had."

She frowned. "A physical scent?"

Idryll waved dismissively. "Physical, magical, whatever. They're all senses to me. I can tell you that they're connected."

A surge of excitement went through her. "Then we know where to look. So I guess we *are* going hunting after all."

CHAPTER TWENTY-SEVEN

The day had passed in a blur. Idryll had growled about being left behind, mentioning boredom and claws, but Ruby wasn't prepared to explain to her human mentor why she felt the need to carry a cat around all day. She'd visited Margrave and discussed some gadgets she'd need in the future, plus one that she needed right away. He'd raised a suspicious eyebrow when she'd asked if he knew anyone who did work with magic and clothes but had given her a couple of names to check out. *No time for it now, but if I'm going to continue to cause trouble out in public, I need a disguise that doubles as protection, to protect the ones I love and myself.*

After that, she'd asked Demetrius to stay by the phone that evening in case. He, too, clearly had questions but didn't ask them. Then she'd portaled to Oriceran to meet with Keshalla, not even taking the time to dress appropriately before heading out to find her.

Her mentor sat on one of the boulders in the grassy field, her eyes closed and her head tilted up to enjoy the breeze. Nonetheless, Ruby hadn't gotten any closer than thirty feet before her teacher said, "Welcome, *minari*."

She didn't reply until she was seated on the nearest boulder, about six feet away from the other woman. "Greetings, *shenai*."

"What vexes you?" Keshalla always seemed to know what Ruby felt. Eventually, she'd quit trying to figure out how and decided it was probably magic and she shouldn't worry about it.

"Two mysteries. First, I returned from my *venamisha* with a companion. A shapeshifter. I don't know why." She was relieved that most of the words she wanted to say came out, as they'd utterly failed to do with her parents, but also frustrated that the remainder, specifically the information about Idryll, didn't. "I also don't know why I can talk about it with you, but not with others."

The other woman grinned. "The relationship between *minari* and *shenai* is itself a magical one. This does not surprise me. However, you gaining a partner does." She looked thoughtful and slowly nodded. "I have never heard of such a thing, although perhaps it is because you are my first student to undergo the trial, at least that I'm aware of. I can only say that if you've been paired, your other half will play a pivotal role in your future."

Ruby groaned. "Wow. That's really clear. I feel so much more understanding than I did a couple of minutes ago." She hoped her sarcasm was thick enough to convey her true feelings. "Second mystery, then. Two acts of violence in my city without a clear reason."

"Indeed. You have a role in this why?"

She shrugged. "Because I was there for the first, and

now feel a responsibility to those who died to make it right."

Keshalla opened her eyes and trained them on her. "The dead do not care."

"The living they left behind do. Someone needs to speak for them."

"Is that not why you have law officers?"

Ruby sighed. "In this case, they don't seem to be particularly effective. There's a sheriff who I think cares a lot, but I can't be seen nosing around in this. Some feel I might be involved in these acts."

Her teacher's lips twisted into a frown, and her voice dropped a notch. "Why would they believe such a thing?" The evident threat in her tone would scare anyone smart enough to understand it.

"Because of my family. Some think negative events at other casinos can be considered positive ones for us."

"Nonsense. You would never act with such a lack of honor."

Ruby laughed. "Not everyone holds me in as high a regard as you do."

Keshalla snorted. "Well, they should. Now, why did you wish to see me?"

"Advice." The other woman nodded, an invitation for her to continue. "I face an unknown number of enemies, and cannot afford to reveal myself. I have a disguise, but it's less than optimal. I don't dare wear anything that identifies me as a Mist Elf, either. I hoped you might have suggestions for how I should arm myself for the fight ahead."

She smiled, the sort of expression that promised danger

—danger for Ruby's enemies. "Indeed, in this I can assist. Come." They made their way to Keshalla's home, where the older woman gave her suggestions and advice on how she might best act with subtlety in the current situation. Ruby had expected to enter the armory as usual, but instead, her teacher opened the basement door and led her below to a chamber she'd never seen.

Thick stone blocks made up the house's foundation, and to judge by the lack of dampness in the underground space, were probably spelled to keep moisture out and maintain a comfortable, if slightly chilly, temperature. The room was a sizeable rectangle, empty of anything other than weapon racks and a trio of large concentric circles in the center of the space. The outermost was silver, the one right next to it, gold, and the small one in the middle, only wide enough to accommodate two or three people standing close together, was made of diamond. Ruby gasped, and Keshalla laughed. "You act as though you've never seen a diamond before."

"A diamond, yes. An unbroken ring of solid diamond… I never imagined such a thing could exist."

"Despite all you have learned already, there is a great deal more of the world than you have seen. Remember that, and tread lightly as you go." It sounded more like prophecy than advice, the way she said it. "Now, let's see to solving your immediate problem. Fatal, or nonfatal?"

Ruby blinked, then realized what she was asking. "Unfortunately, some of each, I would say. I would hope they don't force me into killing, but I can't speak for those on the other side."

Keshalla nodded. "Then you will have sticks with

retractable blades and your sword, plus knives." Ruby thought to complain that she didn't need that many but reconsidered. *I'll wind up with more if I do that.* As if she'd heard the thought, her teacher added, "This is only due to the short notice, of course. When the current crisis is over, we will re-evaluate these choices."

Ruby crossed the circles to stand beside the other woman as she opened a cabinet to reveal weapons that were familiar but not identical to the ones she'd trained with. "Drow weapons," Keshalla explained. "Very similar in most ways but visually different. Should hide both your human and Mist Elf heritage from anyone who would recognize them. Plus, our arts are enough alike that it would take someone deeply experienced with one or the other to tell them apart."

She handed over the sticks. They were made of a black wood that seemed heavier than it should be and set with small gemstones along the length that, while certainly decorative, would also hurt a lot if they hit someone. Ruby flicked them in a way that should have brought out the blades, but none appeared. She tried again, then growled, "Little help here?"

Her teacher laughed. "You have to thread some magic into them to release or retract the blade."

Ruby frowned and did so, and a sharp-edged piece of metal clicked into place on each of the four "sides" of the cylindrical weapon. She whipped it around, pleased with the continued balance. Another push of magic and the blades retracted. Keshalla handed over a pair of black sheaths that would strap onto her thighs to hold the weapons and turned back to the cabinet. "One day we will have to talk about the exquisite skill of Drow dagger work. For now, these will serve you well."

Her teacher offered a knife next, the blade about as long as the space between Ruby's elbow and wrist. The pommel was simple leather-wrapped metal, and the balance was again exquisite. The killing part of the weapon was straight with a strange raised channel down the middle that she'd never seen before. She pointed at it. "This?"

Keshalla shrugged. "For poison. I can provide some if you like, but without additional training, it could pose a risk to you as well."

"Uh, no, thanks, I'm good." The other woman laughed and handed over the blade's twin and a pair of sheaths that would fit the daggers at each hip, held by a black leather belt with curls and whorls tooled into it. Then she provided a pair of thin throwing knives and boot sheaths for them. Finally, she withdrew a sword and gave it to her.

Ruby took a step back not to endanger the other woman and drew the blade from its holder. It was thinner than the ones she'd trained with and had a slight upward curve to it. It was engraved from tip to hilt in symbols she didn't recognize. She sliced it gently through the air and admired its balance. "This is a little different than ours."

Keshalla nodded. "The Drow are more finesse-focused than we are. While our style would be described by many as indirect, compared to those folks, we're straight-punchers." She laughed. "These weapons will serve you well, and more importantly, will confuse your enemies."

Ruby accepted the sheath that would position the sword on her back with a smile. "A wise woman once told me, confusing our enemies is much to be desired. Then told me again. About a thousand times."

Her teacher laughed. "Well, if my student had any sort of memory, perhaps such repetition wouldn't be necessary." She affectionately tapped Ruby on the head.

"If you hit your student in the head less often, perhaps her memory would be better."

Keshalla lifted an eyebrow. "If you guarded better, perhaps not so many strikes would land on such a vulnerable area."

Ruby raised her hands in defeat. "All right. You win. I surrender."

"Fight well, *minari*. Bring honor on yourself, and thus on me."

The corollary, not to embarrass her teacher, was unstated but clear. "Count on it."

That night found Ruby and Idryll outside the security company again, but this time high up on the hill that overlooked it. The gadget she'd borrowed from Margrave was based on a high-quality long-distance microphone. He'd added magic to it that amplified the volume considerably and allowed it to detect through solid objects that would normally muffle the sound waves. The magic sensed the sounds and replicated them again and again, capturing even the softest. In the hands of a human, it would work well. In hers, she'd be able to use her magic to improve the results substantially.

They'd packed snacks and dressed appropriately for the

evening. Ruby was ready to stay there overnight, hiding under a veil, and all the next day if required. She'd wait and listen until she got a clue about what was going on, and if she could, she'd blow them up. *Not literally, although that might be the easiest solution. I'm sure Idryll would approve.* The duffel bag with their costumes and her weapons sat nearby. She was ready for whatever might happen. She'd had the foresight to lock down the room that connected the kemana to Spirit for the night, so if she needed to portal back she could do so in safety without risking discovery.

Ruby tuned in the microphone and heard several voices talking over one another. The rustle of clothing and equipment and the occasional overly loud laugh told her something was up. She whispered, "There's a bunch of them in there." She checked her watch, and it confirmed that it was ten-thirty. Her expectation had been for a quiet night with only guard patrols to listen to and a long day of trying to pick up clues, but they'd found something else.

She switched off the feed to the small earpiece and turned on the speaker low, and together they bent to listen.

CHAPTER TWENTY-EIGHT

Grentham paced in the locker room at Aces Security. The job was going down with too much haste, and the fact that the boss would only communicate with Trenton meant that he had no opportunity to talk anyone out of it. *They're all getting really excited about themselves. That lasts right until the first big reversal. If this goes wrong, it's going to be ugly.*

Of course, the head of Aces couldn't possibly be involved. He was out on yet another date and being seen, making sure he had an alibi so nothing could be traced back to him. The dwarf knew he was repeatedly positioned as a fall guy if the house of cards they were building fell, and while he couldn't do anything about that within the company, anyone coming after him would find their quarry much more difficult to catch than they'd ever anticipated.

Which doesn't help matters now, at all. He had handpicked the ten men who would accompany him today. They'd worked under the table for Aces before, so there wouldn't be a direct connection unless one of them talked. He was satisfied that none would. If he were wrong, the fact that they were wired into the police and correctional departments would mean he'd hear about it fast enough to make sure that the snitch never made it to a deposition. He was working on something implantable, some piece of magic or technology that would eliminate people at a whim, but it was more a pet project than anything real, and he didn't have time for many of those. *I should probably stop re-watching* Escape from New York *for a while.*

His crew was dressed in black and armed with pistols and rifles taken from criminals by the Reno police. Someday they'd discover that the small arsenal had mysteriously vanished from their evidence lockup. The clothes had been mail-ordered to a PO box and paid for by a shell company. Then a hired infomancer made sure the transaction disappeared. Fortunately, he'd taken those precautions some time before in anticipation of the day when he'd be thrust into a situation like this.

He stopped pacing and put his hands on his hips, judging that everyone was appropriately dressed and ready to go. "Okay, people, here's the deal. We have a rare opportunity, which is why we rolled this thing out in such a hurry. A family that owns one of the casinos hasn't been interested in working with us although some recent events should've convinced them otherwise. Well, we're going to reinforce that message tonight. They're holding a street festival celebrating the opening of a new restaurant in their fancy business. Handing out samples to average folk like us, I suspect."

The men in the room laughed, and he grinned at the confirmation that he knew the right buttons to push. "We're going to take a little more than the samples. The two owners have only one child, a teenager, college boy down in Vegas. The goal is simple. We crash the party, take the kid, and hold him for ransom."

His people showed a mixture of surprise, shock, and eager anticipation. "The best part is that the payoff isn't the thing I'm looking for. So whatever we get, you all split evenly." *As far as you know, anyway.*

That got their attention. One asked, "How much we talking?"

Grentham shrugged. "Three hundred thousand each, minus expenses. So, between two-point-five and three." Cheers and a couple of high fives came in response. They were ready. "Rental vehicles are already in position for the escape, and we've prepped the safe house where we're taking him. We'll roll out in the company's vans and walk the last mile or so. The big event is at midnight, so we have to get moving."

Up on the hillside, Ruby and Idryll looked at each other in shock. The tiger-woman observed, "This is an evil plan."

"No more evil than what they've been up to so far, I guess." She shoved the stuff in the bag and pulled out their costumes. "The good news is, we can get there first."

Idryll took her outfit and quickly climbed into it. Ruby did the same, minus the mask, and made sure her illusory face was present. She summoned a portal that would take them to an alley near the Kraken, the casino owned by the Atlantean contingent in Magic City. Their new restaurant —seafood, obviously—had been the talk of the town for weeks during its by-invitation-only soft opening. Tonight, they were figuratively throwing their arms wide to invite everyone to taste their celebrity chef's cuisine.

She waited a few seconds to see if anyone on the other side noticed the rift and stepped through. Then she created another portal, this time into the nondescript locked room at Spirit, and threw the bag with their ordinary clothes through. Idryll asked, "What's the plan?"

Ruby replied, "No one would believe us if we told them they were in danger, so we'll have to wait for things to kick off and protect the Chentashe family."

The tiger-woman nodded. "Am I free to kill the attackers?"

There it was. Ruby had walked the tightrope of that question all along and now had to pick a side to fall on. She relied on the words of her teacher and echoed them to her partner. "Where talking will do, talk; where wounding will do, wound; but if killing is necessary, do not hesitate."

Idryll nodded. "My philosophy as well. Except for the middle part." She grinned and drew a laugh from Ruby.

"You suck." She sidled forward with her back against the wall toward the alley mouth while putting a veil over them both. Hidden, she donned her mask, readying to defend as many innocents as she could. *I wish I had a tracking device. I should have brought the drone.* A hundred other "should haves" crossed her mind at that moment, but the truth was that it had all happened too fast. *When this is over, I'm going to prepare properly in case this garbage ever happens again. Better suit, more weapons, and a safe place to work from where I won't endanger my family or friends.*

They couldn't get too far out into the crowd without

risking someone bumping into them. The illusion only worked against the eyes, and the laws of physics still applied. She found the best angle she could to keep them safe and focused inward, pulling her magic up. It was something she'd always naturally done that she'd learned was a good thing when she'd started training with Keshalla. Her powers would respond a little quicker if she built them in advance, and every part-second would give her an advantage in battle. She was thoroughly disgusted that the scumbags in the security company had decided to go after a kid. *Sure, he'd probably be offended to be described that way, but he's still not old enough to drink. That feels like it ought to be off-limits.*

She didn't doubt the Atlanteans' ability to see to their defense, but if the attackers were smart, they'd occupy the parents while they snatched the child. Proper planning would go a long way toward managing their goal. Her tension rose as the owners stepped up to the podium together and announced the new restaurant, then gestured for the celebrity chef to come up and speak. She did so, and cheers and whistles sounded in the crowd, all of whom seemed to have indulged a little before the event. *That'll add to the chaos.*

Idryll whispered, "I taste magic." Ruby wrapped them each in force shields an inch from their skin, and put a conical bubble around them, one foot on each side and one foot above their heads. The opening salvo of the attack hit a moment later. A fanfare of explosions went off directly across the thoroughfare, drawing attention in that direction. Fortunately, they didn't seem to be demolitions, only fireworks, light, and sound. The crowd cheered as the display continued, thinking it was part of the event. Then a sudden shimmering gave way to a group of black-suited men holding rifles. They pulled the triggers, sending a barrage of bullets toward the stage as the people on it screamed.

Ruby was ready. She dropped the veil and summoned a force shield across the front of the firing line to absorb the bullets. She felt each hit like it was a tiny punch, but it wasn't enough to distract her—or to stop her from rushing at the nearest attacker. Idryll was already in the air, leaping to get into the middle of the group. The man swiveled toward her, and she called up another force shield, angling it so the rounds would deflect harmlessly up over the stage roof. He emptied his magazine. The impacts tired her and drained her power, but she was on him before he could reload. A punch to the face followed by a rising kick to the groin and a jump kick to the chest took him out and knocked the man behind him off-balance.

She never saw the object that smashed into the back of her head. Her first warning was the impact, which blasted stars through her vision and sent her stumbling to the ground at the feet of the rifle-wielding men.

CHAPTER TWENTY-NINE

Idryll saw Ruby go down and instantly realized she had only one option to keep the riflemen from killing her partner. Clothes tore as her form changed, and where there had been a woman in a catsuit, a tiger now stood in her place, half again as large as anything seen on this planet, and deeply angry at the injury to one she called her own.

She leapt forward, slammed into the ones nearest her partner, and carried them to the ground. They faced too many enemies to be totally merciful, but she minimized the damage the best she could, stomping on their shoulder blades to break them and prevent the men from using their arms should they have thoughts of rejoining the battle.

Three had fallen, another three were near her, and four had advanced toward the stage. She felt the presence of magic and threw herself to the side, narrowly avoiding a blast of shadow. She was most vulnerable to that magic type in her present form, which wasn't to say it rendered her powerless. *Neither do I wish to be hit with it, however.* She ran to intercept the men heading for the stage, but a sudden wash of fire interposed itself, and she skidded to a halt. Her head snapped around, and she spotted the magical attacker and charged, but the short figure called up a veil and slipped out of view.

Idryll slashed at the nearest man, knocking his legs out from underneath him and gashing his thigh. Blood spurted, and he hurriedly grabbed a medical pouch at his waist. She let him do it, not willing to kill unless she had to —or unless Ruby truly was hurt, in which case she would eliminate every enemy she saw, upright or not. A shimmer in the air revealed the magical again, a dwarf with black hair. He'd gotten an angle on Ruby, so Idryll did the only thing she could do and charged into the space between them.

Ruby had reached her feet, but her eyes were still trying to focus when the sizzling forks of lightning slammed into the tiger who had jumped in front of her. She felt drained, having expended more magic to keep the shields up than she could remember using, maybe ever. She was grateful for the foresight that caused her to use her mask rather than relying on her ability to maintain an illusion. However, the tiger writhing on the ground needed her help. Expending almost all of her remaining magic, she created a portal to Spirit and used a force blast to push Idryll through right before her power to keep it open was spent.

Even without her magic, Ruby was a formidable fighter. She drew her sword and jumped up to the stage, where the Atlanteans were shielding against the rifle fire from the remaining men on the ground. A trio of enemies had made it to the platform, and she charged them. Their reluctance to shoot when they didn't have a clear angle that avoided the Atlanteans made her realize that even the men shooting below were misdirections. The goal wasn't to kill the parents or the child, only to kidnap the boy. *Damn it Ruby, get the gods-damned cotton out of your brain.* They pulled batons, but there was no way they would be good enough to defeat her even three-to-one. She traded blows with the first, blocked a punch and a swipe of the baton, then smashed him in the face with her sword hilt.

He went down, and she took a thrust from the next one's baton in the chest. The stun blast locked up her muscles for an instant, and he threw a punch at her that connected with her cheek and sent her stumbling. As soon as she was free from the baton, her anger overwhelmed any pain. She snatched a throwing knife and hurled it at him. The weapon buried itself in his thigh, causing him to scream and clutch his leg before he went down. The next one waved the baton threateningly but didn't advance, waiting for her to make the first move.

She caught the oncoming attack out of the corner of her eye, hit the ground, and rolled under the stream of shadow bolts that sought her. She'd seen the dwarf and looked forward to paying him back for the magical sucker-punch he'd given her. Then the man on the stage pelted away, and the shadow attacks stopped. The rifle fire started up again, and the Atlanteans finally dove for cover, apparently their defenses also weakening under the barrage. She saw then that only two of them were still on the stage. *Shit. They got the kid. That's why the change in tactics.*

Grentham ran ahead of the black-suited man who was dragging the Atlantean brat along beside him. He'd had to slap the boy once to make him quit struggling, but now he was mostly obeying. The dwarf had long ago gotten over the fact that he had to run to keep pace with a fast-walking human, but tonight it was particularly annoying. He'd expected resistance, but whoever the hell the weirdo in the red leather was, she and her tiger were way more trouble than anyone could have anticipated.

Still, I got the better of them both. He chuckled, accustomed to winning but still quite capable of enjoying it immensely when it happened. Once they were in the van, the man would drive and he'd watch over the kid, maybe slap him around a little more for fun. He'd lost track of how many of his men had gone down, but they all had instructions: if they couldn't make it to the safe house, they should scatter after the operation and get in contact a week later for payment.

He hoped the family would pay up quickly so they could get this over with before the Feds got involved. Since they'd visibly used magic, the Paranormal Defense Agency would be on the case, and kidnappings sometimes fell to the Federal Bureau of Investigation, especially for high-profile abductions. *We don't need their attention.* He got to the van and opened the back doors in time for the other man to throw the kid inside. He climbed up, grabbed the roll of duct tape, and quickly bound the boy's hands and legs.

The doors closed with a *clang*, and moments later the van pulled out of the parking lot, headed for the safe house. Neither of the men could see the woman hanging on the back, who carefully avoided both the windows and the backup camera. If they'd been able to read her mind, they would have heard a repeated mantra: "This is so stupid. This is so stupid. This is so stupid."

Ruby slipped off the back and scrambled to get underneath the vehicle when the van reached its destination. The surface below was gravel, and she'd seriously scratched her hands and the exposed parts of her face by the time she finished. She heard the men pull their captive out and watched their feet as they dragged him to a doorway in a metal-skinned building and took him through.

She paused, torn between staying in her current position and moving. A little of her magical energy had returned, enough to shield if she needed to, but she wasn't willing to trust her life to a potentially short-term veil if she could help it. The fact that the dust in her nose threatened to make her sneeze was the deciding factor. She scrambled out on the far side of the vehicle, then stood and brushed herself off, getting more scratches for her trouble. She peered over the hood and saw a dilapidated warehouse, about two stories high, with small square windows in frames covering the second level. Many of them were broken, and she could picture kids using them for target practice.

There will be a ladder somewhere. That's what I need. She ran for the nearest edge of the building, which happened to be on her left, and circled the structure until she found what she was looking for. It terminated ten feet off the ground, but she had enough juice to use a small force blast to send her up to it. She grabbed the bottom rung and hauled herself up, then climbed to the top. The roof was disgusting, covered with sticky tar and bird droppings and the remains of rodents. Still, it had what she hoped for, skylights at regular intervals.

Her brain pushed her to rush over and verify the captive was okay, but she forced herself to pause and breathe. She opened her senses as she had during her *venamisha*, searching for any signs of magic, fearful that the dwarf—who either had to be Grentham or the greatest coincidence *ever*—had prepared the hideout with the thought of intruders. She sensed nothing though, and crept carefully along, peering into each skylight before moving to the next. At the last, she saw the dwarf and the black-suited man standing outside a small building constructed within the warehouse. She could hear them mocking the boy, who was presumably in the smaller structure. *So, that's good news since it means they're probably not planning to move him again right away.*

The bad news was the two lines of simple metal beds, which suggested more people would be there soon. Worse, maybe, was the stockpile of supplies in a corner that said they'd prepared to be there for a while. *No time. If I call in the police, it'll be a shootout. If I let it go, there's no guarantee they won't kill the kid after making the deal, especially since he's seen them.* She pulled the energy potion out of her pocket and drank it, then gasped with pleasure as magical power flowed into her. They were incredibly expensive, so they were always the last resort, but if she ever had a good reason to take one, this was it. She twisted and sent a bolt of force magic at the farthest skylight, shattering it, then jumped through the nearest one, a buffer of force magic leading the way.

Her distraction didn't work as well as she'd hoped. The gunman looked elsewhere, but she hadn't fooled the dwarf. He made a punching motion and a ball of force slammed into her shield, the impact powerful enough to send her flying. Ruby used her magic to cushion the fall, then rolled to her feet, ready to fight. Bullets cut through the air at her. She pictured a circular shield attached to her left arm, and one appeared in shimmering force. She positioned it to intercept the bullets, deflecting them rather than directly opposing them to minimize the defense's magical cost. The other hand threw attacks, first lightning, then fire, then cold, all of which the dwarf intercepted with bursts of power.

Ruby growled inwardly at the stalemate, knowing that eventually the gunman would get lucky and she'd wind up losing. She expanded the force shield and made it opaque, then crouched behind it. She drew her last throwing knife and simultaneously dispelled the protection and hurled herself into the air with a force blast. Her arm whipped forward as she threw the blade at the man with the gun. It caught him right where the shoulder connected to the neck, where the armor didn't protect, and sank deep into his flesh. The move cost her as the dwarf blasted her with lightning, tracking her twitching body as it fell to the floor.

Ruby gritted her teeth as he advanced, fearful he would try a more lethal distance attack but knowing in her gut he'd want to be close for the finishing blow. When he finally stood over her, he said something she couldn't hear, some sort of insult no doubt, and gathered his power for a final blast. She smiled and whispered, "*Kagji.*" A shield of shadow formed around her, created by the amulet that Keshalla had given her during the *venamisha*, which she'd worn at all times since.

She planted her left foot and twisted her hips, kicking him in the hand with her heavy boot hard enough to break bones. *Yeah, let's see how your fancy gestures work now, asshole.* She flipped up as he backpedaled and threw magic with his offhand, but her shield still felt strong. She drew her sword from over her shoulder, confident that if anyone she'd fought so far deserved to die, it was the dwarf. She saw first fear in his eyes, then quick calculation, and realized what he would do as he did it. Fire magic exploded in a semicircle around him, a wave of force and heat that hit her shield and did nothing, and that would probably have incinerated the hostage if she hadn't reached out with her telekinesis and slammed the door of his shelter closed.

Screams came from inside the room, and she had to choose: check on the boy or follow the dwarf, who ran all-out toward the door. She chose the former and found him inside, singed but alive. Some of the fire magic had gotten in through the cracks and crevices in the less-well-built-than-she'd-thought holding pen. She calmed him, then stuck her head out the door to find only the fallen guard remained. He was panting, deeply in pain, and his pallor was worrisome. Ruby pulled out her burner phone and hit Demetrius' number. "Send the cops to my location. Got it?"

"Got it. Cops on the way to your current position," then rattled off coordinates like she'd know what the hell they meant. *Goofball.* She shook her head and turned back to the Atlantean.

"Police are coming. I'll be nearby watching until they get here, in case more of these scumbags show up." She grabbed the fallen man's pistol, popped the magazine to check that it was loaded, slid it back into place, and gave the gun to the boy. "He comes toward you, shoot him."

The one she'd been thinking of as a boy because of how the dwarf had referred to him was a notably handsome young man with his dark eyes and snaky dreadlocks. He nodded. "Will do. Thank you, uh, cat person."

Ruby laughed and had to stop herself from losing it entirely. "Right. Be good." She dashed for the door to the sound of distant sirens coming closer. *Be good? Really? No wonder you're not currently dating anyone with lines like that.*

CHAPTER THIRTY

It had taken almost a full day before Idryll was willing to talk to her again. Ruby wasn't sure if it was because she was upset at Ruby's lack of skill, or she was hurt and hiding it, or she was mad because Ruby had kicked her out of the fight, or all of the above. When the tiger-woman finally spoke, all she would say about the battle was, "We need to train together, to work as a team."

"Can't argue with that," Ruby replied, and things had slowly warmed up from there. She'd visited with her family and her roommates and discussed the amazing events of the night before with each. Of course, Ruby had supposedly missed it all, having been asleep in her bed at the time. Her parents thought she'd been at the house above the surface. Her roommates thought she'd been below. *Neat and tidy.*

She patted Idryll on the leg as they shared a boulder in her Oriceran village. "Everything wrapped up perfectly well. Now I can get back to working on the important stuff, like getting a job. Hopefully, things will be calm from here on out."

The tiger-woman snorted. She was clad in fur, having refused to wear other clothing on her home planet. Ruby had stuck with jeans and a t-shirt rather than dressing in her appropriate clothes. It was a day of much-needed rest, a pause to let the world settle in the proper direction again before she started setting up the stuff she'd need to start her business for real. Idryll said, "You really believe that, don't you?"

Ruby straightened her spine from where she'd been leaning back and said, "No, not really. But I can hope, right?"

Idryll's eyes flicked over her shoulder, and she turned to see Keshalla approaching. The tiger-woman asked, "What do you think, Lady Keshalla?"

Ruby frowned. *Lady Keshalla? What's up with that?* Her teacher replied, "I believe that my student is leaving many questions unanswered in her supposed desire to get on with what she considers a normal life."

Her frown turned into a scowl. "Hey, first, how about you don't talk about me like I'm not here? Second, what questions do you mean?"

Idryll nodded, then replied as if she hadn't spoken. "Normal. Yes, that explains much. She can never have such a thing."

Keshalla said, "No, she can't."

Ruby growled, "Will one of you please explain? Like, now?"

The tiger-woman said, "Two issues are relevant. First, you are a special person, Ruby Achera. You were called to the *venamisha*. You are destined for far more than a 'normal' life. Many paths that you will travel have yet to reveal themselves."

She rolled her eyes. "Okay, Obi-Wan. Whatever you say."

Keshalla added, "The second issue is that you have not yet solved the mystery you set out to solve. You foiled the kidnapping, true, but have you identified everyone involved in the plot? More importantly, have you answered why they did it? Until you've resolved these, you cannot be truly finished."

Ruby sighed. "Yeah. I get it. You know what this means, right? It's going to be so much work. I need a new outfit, better gadgets, a place to operate from. People, don't you understand that I'm naturally lazy?"

Her teacher laughed, as did her partner. Keshalla asked, "Do you feel you've achieved justice for those who were killed?"

Ruby sobered immediately. "No. No, I haven't."

Idryll nodded. "We still have things to accomplish. We'll do them together."

"Are you saying I'm stuck with you?"

The tiger-woman grinned, showing off sharp fangs. "Indeed. No, you don't have a choice in the matter. The *venamisha* chose for you."

Ruby acknowledged the inevitable with a sigh. "All right. I give up. You two better have some good ideas about all this stuff though because I'm right out of them at the moment."

Keshalla grinned. "Ah, *minari*. Your work has only

begun. However, we will be with you every step of the way."

Grentham had been yelling at him for almost a half-hour, and Jared had about reached the end of his tolerance for it. He knew his partner was volatile at the best of times and had guessed he would be offended when Jared didn't participate in the kidnapping operation. Still, neither of those things was relevant because his boss wanted Aces Security to stay clean, so he would continue to avoid being linked to the crime spree in Magic City.

The dwarf, his voice hoarse, demanded, "Tell me that we won't do anything on that short notice again. Commit to it. Have some backbone, man."

Jared laughed. "When you feel like you can say that to the boss, you can be in charge, and I'll be your number two. *I'm* sure as hell not going to do it. I'm going to continue to say, 'Yes sir, how high, sir?' You let me know when you want to do differently."

His phone rang, and Jared frowned at it, then his heart started beating triple time as he saw who it was. He answered. "Yes. Uh-huh. Yes. Thirty minutes. Yes," and hung up. He looked over at the dwarf, his mouth dry. "It, uh, looks like you'll get your chance. We have an appointment with the boss."

They both downed a shot of whiskey for luck, then Jared drove them through the darkness to a place he'd never been before, an intersection out in the desert with an old and abandoned gas station on one corner. A stretch limo sat there, and four dark-suited men with guns stood at each corner of it, all of them tracking their approach. He and the dwarf stepped out slowly, and each of them was thoroughly and professionally searched by one of the guards while the others kept weapons trained on them.

Finally, one of them opened the limo's rear door and waved them inside. A man and a woman sat there, the former in a stylish and expensive business suit and tie, the latter in a notably tight dress suitable for a night out on the town. Jared took the spot farther from the door and saw Grentham wince as he sat.

Gabriel Sloane was known to his enemies as The Nightmare, a moniker that hearkened back to his time as an enforcer and assassin. After making a bundle in those occupations, he'd killed his way to the top of a small criminal organization, then absorbed several others through tactics both businesslike and brutal. To Jared and Grentham, he was "Boss," or occasionally "Big Man," or "Him."

Sloane was angry, to judge by the twist of his lips. "I find myself concerned by your incompetence, gentlemen. So much so that my wife and I will be late to a party in our honor so that we can have this conversation. Oh, and Mister Grentham, by now you've felt the anti-magic emitter. Please don't get any ideas about trying to overcome it."

The dwarf nodded. Jared replied, "We experienced unexpected complications in the last two attempts, sir. Someone is acting against us. We've already begun tracing—"

The man lifted a hand to stop him, and Jared's voice died. His superior resembled what George Clooney might look like if someone grabbed his face and stretched it vertically. He was handsome but looked somehow wrong. *Or maybe that's the eyes, which are as crazy as I've ever seen on anyone other than his wife.* Jared wasn't afraid of much, but he was scared of these two.

Sloane said, "Here's what's going to happen. You'll continue working the angles we've planned, but more slowly. I'm planning to bring in some out-of-town talent and take the game up a notch. When he's finished, these aliens ought to run to you for protection. Once you're inside, it will be child's play to make them do what I want."

"Yes, sir," Jared replied. He still couldn't figure what the man's endgame was. He was already rich, and there had to be a lot of better ways to get richer. At first, he'd thought it might simply be the pleasure of playing a game that was valuable because it was out of reach of anyone with less money or more ethics. It felt like something more was going on in the background though, something that he might understand if he could make the right mental shift. "It might help to either acquire our competition or, uh, encourage them to leave the business."

"I have no interest in the former. However, if you have plans to accomplish the latter that don't take away from the tasks I've assigned you, by all means, strengthen your position." He tapped a button on the console next to him, and the door opened. Jared and Grentham climbed out and turned respectfully back toward the limo. Sloane leaned over. "One more thing. Any more failures, and it'll cost you far more than a conversation. Keep that in mind."

Jared kept it in mind all the way back to Magic City. As he dropped Grentham off, he saw the other man thought similarly. "We need to get rid of whoever's after us, first thing."

The dwarf nodded. "Agreed. No more playing nice. We find them, we make sure they pay in blood for getting in our way, and we kill them."

The city she thought she knew was a lie... can Ruby find a way to save it before time runs out? Find out in *A MAGICAL ALLIANCE.*

If you enjoyed this book, you may also enjoy the first series from T.R. Cameron, also set in the Oriceran Universe. The Federal Agents of Magic series begins with Magic Ops and it's available now at Amazon and through Kindle Unlimited.

FBI Agent Diana Sheen is an agent with a secret...

...She carries a badge and a troll, along with a little magic.

But her Most Wanted List is going to take a little extra effort.

She'll have to embrace her powers and up her game to take down new threats,

Not to mention deal with the troll that's adopted her.

All signs point to a serious threat lurking just beyond sight, pulling the strings to put the forces of good in harm's way.

Magic or mundane, you break the law, and Diana's gonna find you, tag you and bring you in. Watch out magical baddies, this agent can level the playing field.

It's all in a day's work for the newest Federal Agent of Magic.

Available now at Amazon and through Kindle Unlimited

Back in the Oriceran Universe with a bang! (See what I did there? Because of the explosion at the casino? Nevermind.) I hope you enjoyed Book 1. So much adventure lies ahead as we explore the various sights and sounds of Magic City and see Ruby come into her own as its magical defender. Not to mention figuring out what the venamisha portends, other than the addition of an inordinately sassy companion.

I had a lot of fun with this one. It was great stepping back into Urban Fantasy. My return to Sci-Fi for the Azophi series was great, but it reminded me that this is where I feel most comfortable. I like the trappings of our current world, but with a twist.

In future books, several of the characters who got fairly little "screen time" in this one will become more important, and there will be some visits from characters that those have been with me since Magic Ops will no doubt enjoy seeing again. I am eternally grateful that Martha and

Michael have let me stake my claim to a corner of the Oriceran Universe and weave in and out of what they've done while adding my own elements as well.

I am really jazzed about exploring the magical item creation angle on things in this series. Coming up with new and clever objects is a mental challenge all on its own, and finding a way to seamlessly incorporate them in the story another. I have long enjoyed seeing that sort of thing in the books I write, though. At this moment, I'm remembering a character named Cadderly, from Salvatore's cleric quintet, and a crossbow with exploding bolts. (I hope I'm remembering that right). I loved that, and adding in magic will make it all the more fun in Magic City.

It's worth mentioning that Ely, Nevada, really exists, but has little in common with the version I'm using here. My research makes it seem like a pretty cool place, though. The train museum is a real thing. There are mountains nearby. But otherwise, there's a ton of dramatic license there. Although, who's to say there's *not* a Kemana underneath, really?

Life outside writing is a mix of joy and frustration, as I'm sure it is for everyone. The kid and I missed out on our summer of amusement parks, which bummed the both of us out considerably. We're playing Fortnite together, working slowly through *Avengers* on the PS4, and have just started playing with World of Warcraft again. My wife and I were, uh, well, let's just call it what it is – seriously addicted to that game for a while there, back when it was new. And with a new expansion about to come out, we're playing the trial to see if the kiddo likes it enough that we should dive in again. And while I thought I'd be playing Cyberpunk 2077 by now, at least it's only been pushed back to December 10, so only a few weeks!

Watching *Picard*, waiting for the *Expanse*, and consuming a lot of so-bad-they're-almost-good movies. Also slowly moving through season 1 of the *Mandalorian* again before advancing to season 2. Heavens above, that show is *slow*.

The two new kittens are now fully integrated into the household. Going from five to seven seems like an exponential increase. There is *always* a cat, no matter what you happen to be doing. One of them has jumped in the shower with the kid twice now. The other loves taking a bath in the sink while drinking water from the faucet. But they're both sweet and cuddly, at least if you get them when they're tired and not racing through the house like cheetah / mountain goat hybrids. Although watching the two of them chasing after the older cats is pretty darn entertaining.

The kid and I are still watching movies in the car a few evenings a week. Most recently, the animated Addams family movie, which was laugh out loud enjoyable.

If this is your first taste of my Urban Fantasy, look for "Magic Ops." I promise you'll enjoy it. You might also enjoy my science fiction work. All my writing is filled with action, snark, and villains who think they're heroes. Drop by www.trcameron.com and take a look!

Until next time, Joys upon joys to you and yours – so may it be.

PS: If you'd like to chat with me, here's the place. I check in daily or more: https://www.facebook.com/ AuthorTRCameron. Often I put up interesting and/or silly content there, as well. For more info on my books, and to join my reader's group, please visit www.trcameron.com.

I've hit my second wind of clearing out closets and tackling the to-do list. I think it's the approaching end of 2020 and two vaccines out there somewhere. The end of whatever this was is nigh.

If you've been reading a lot of my author notes (and books – so thank you), you would have seen that I kept saying I was going to rid my closet of all clothes I didn't like and can't wear right now. No more aspirational clothes (the ones I hoped I'd fit in some day) and no more just in case clothes (if I grow mysteriously larger). Well, I finally did it. Four green garbage bags and a trip to Goodwill.

I even let go of that camel hair coat with the black collar that I liked so much. I held onto that one like there were no more coats in the world like that one.

Right after I got home, I noticed J. Crew was having a half off coat sale and lo and behold – a lot of coats like that one. Four days later I had a new coat that actually fits and far less 'what ifs' staring me in the face.

There were a couple of surprises after letting go of all

that literal and emotional baggage. I finally saw that I was holding onto clothes that represented a time in Chicago that I loved and wasn't ready to let go of – till now. It was like I wanted it back even though we can't move backward, only forward.

I had been telling myself for years that if I wanted to, I could always go back to Chicago, or back to New York, or even try someplace new. My face was always pressed up against the window wondering what exciting things there are to see out there.

Just traveling to see a place didn't seem like enough.

In the past, when I traveled, I took everything I owned with me. Letting go of all of it was also a way of saying, I'm staying put this time. I'm finally putting down roots and I'm going to let them grow deep, into the ground. Come what may, this is where you'll find me.

It's a new concept for me and may take some getting used to, which is good. All new adventures await from a completely different perspective.

The other surprise was how much I was waiting for things to be different in small and big ways before I was willing to say, I'm happy right now, just as things are. Happy at this size, happy in this house, happy in this town, happy writing these books. The reality is, I am happy but to get rid of that last ounce of restlessness I needed to acknowledge it and act like it.

Since the great clothing purge, I've added handles to the bathrooms, hung more curtains, framed some book covers and put on my office walls and a long list of other things.

I've even signed up for my first kayak lesson and gotten

a portable punching bag. (Quiet Punch – it's amazing, if you want to check it out)

By the time the new year rolls around, I will be ready to go out there and be a part of whatever comes next, without looking back over my shoulder. More adventures to follow.

JOIN THE ORICERAN UNIVERSE FAN GROUP ON FACEBOOK!

BOOKS BY MICHAEL ANDERLE

Sign up for the LMBPN email list to be notified of new releases
and special deals!

https://lmbpn.com/email/

For a complete list of books by Michael Anderle, please visit:

www.lmbpn.com/ma-books/

CONNECT WITH THE AUTHORS

TR Cameron Social

Website: www.trcameron.com

Facebook: https://www.
facebook.com/AuthorTRCameron

Martha Carr Social

Website: http://www.marthacarr.com

Facebook: https://www.facebook.com/
groups/MarthaCarrFans/

Michael Anderle Social

Website: http://lmbpn.com

Email List: http://lmbpn.com/email/

Social Media:

https://www.facebook.com/LMBPNPublishing

https://twitter.com/MichaelAnderle

https://www.instagram.com/lmbpn_publishing/

https://www.bookbub.com/authors/michael-anderle

Made in the USA
Las Vegas, NV
21 October 2023